T0319192

The Birth of a Child in a Fishing Boat

Yemi D. Prince
(Yemi D. Ogunyemi)

Langaa Research & Publishing CIG
Mankon, Bamenda

Publisher
Langaa RPCIG
Langaa Research & Publishing Common Initiative Group
P.O. Box 902 Mankon
Bamenda
North West Region
Cameroon
Langaagrp@gmail.com
www.langaa-rpcig.net

Distributed in and outside N. America by African Books Collective
orders@africanbookscollective.com
www.africanbookscollective.com

ISBN: 9956-763-14-4

DISCLAIMER
All views expressed in this publication are those of the author and do not
necessarily reflect the views of Langaa RPCIG.

Dedication

Dedicated to Chief Reuben O. Ogunyemi and his spouse, Matilda A. Ogunyemi for their undiminished parental support for me during the years of innocence and the promise of pen. My lesson from them lets me know now that Mathematics is everything in life.

Dedicated to Prince Daniel Adebowale, Princess Julia Bosede, Prince Godwin Akintunde, Prince Michael Olukayode and Princess Katharina Omoyemi, for their extra-ordinary patience while Creator-Philosopher Olodumare watches over each one of them.

Acknowledgement

Many thanks to Creator-Philosopher Olodumare for giving me His special grace and courtesy to remember all the events and all the places from the age of two through the age/yeas of innocence till the present. This disproves the theory that to account for facts does not belong to childhood.

Affection emanates from gratitude and appreciation. And gratitude and appreciation are a form of affection. I owe the tripartite to the editors and reviewers of the Langaa Research and Publishing Common Initiative Group, whose vital suggestions and laborious editing and reviewing had made this book to be in print.

I don't want this memoir to go *public*. Why is it that I don't want it to go *public*? It is because I am scared that its unmatched uniqueness will entice the readers to the back of beyond where I was raised with swarms of mosquitoes and tsetse flies struggling for their existence as I was struggling for mine.

Complicating the matter is the revelation implicating my upstanding parents for taking to a piscatorial occupation.

On asking my father to reflect upon what happened during my birth, he harrumphed and said, "There was a zephyr and a breeze in the mangroves and perhaps the mullets were hiding and piping under the lagoonal lilies. All I can add to this is that it was a blessed balmy day—without the blood-sucking insects. While some fishers were busy adjusting their nets and traps, some were in lazy sculls and heaving twos and fours as they waited patiently for the fog to remove its tarpaulin."

Book I

The Birth of a Child in a Fishing Boat

Chapter One

Just As I Was Told

A round me, always there was an air of eternity, tapering to immortality. Eating was immortal. Drinking was immortal. Added to this atmosphere of immortality is how my mother treated me. At the age of two years, I was still sucking her breasts, day and night. Even when I thought I had had enough, I would still drink the milk from her breasts and she would allow me to enjoy the natural enrichment. Sometimes she would spank me and call me a greedy child who would not give its mother a breathing space. She gave me too much of magnanimity and indulgence and little did I know that she was doing all that because of the aura of immortality she had found in me and which is the reason she found it difficult to wean me at the age of two and a half years. In short, breast-feeding is as healthy as it is immortal for the child. This is my personal experience and my magnanimous mother is my witness—my hero—dead or alive. Period.

I know I was borrowing trouble, for even the dashiki upon my back gave me a feeling of immortality. The voice of man as well as the voice of nature was immortal. The voice I heard on a daily basis was immortal because my family and other neighbors, near and far, were immortals. Even Abiku, in its unpredictable, treacherous and, more often than not, annoying ways, was considered a member of the family of immortality.

This is not to assume that I was living in a world of phantasmagoria, for researchers have shown that every child leads an immortal life till the time he/she begins to feel the opposite—feeling the pains of mortality. Added to my picture of immortality are the materials, I could not discard anything: nothing at all was to be discarded. For example, whenever my dashiki was torn, the hole in it would be patched up. The number of holes it had, determined the number of patches it would bear. The hole at the bottom of the bucket would be galvanized. The drum's leather would be mended. The nets would be mended for hours. Once anything was owned, it seemed it would last forever.

In 1954, that air of immortality was punctured when my grandmother yielded to mortality and joined the rank and file of hereafter ancestors. Even with the death of this ancient grandmother, there was little or no doubt in my belief that life is a place of immortality. The folktales and numerous other morality tales point to the verisimilitude based on the Yoruba's strong belief in life and death, and the philosophy that dying is a temporary departure or exit to Creator-Philosopher Olodumare, the Supreme Being who is in His Almighty discretion would turn the dying into a living soul—undying soul.

My belief in immortality is as strong as my belief in day and night. But once I was dead when my parents thought I was alive. I was alive only to let them know I was dead but alive through the benevolence of the most gracious Creator-Philosopher Olodumare, the King of kings and the Lord of lords, the most magnificent, the most loving and the most transparent.

I must let one and all know that my love and marriage with immortality is not a bed of roses for me even when I thought my pie was invariably in the vault of heaven whenever I felt myself comfortably surrounded by the four life-supporting elements—earth, air, fire and water.

Gosh! I was going through a life emblazoned with beauty, love and productivity. I say this and you know why I say this. If I'm repeating this, it is because a life of debauchery was/is not part of my constitution. Life was simply easy, beautiful and in absence of smoking, lying, stealing or committing any other bag-eyed behavior. Naivety and innocence were my closest companions, my un-licked chums. My sole Achilles' heel was infatuation. No one could exonerate me from this ebb, even God in his loving-kindness would refuse to give me a diploma of exoneration.

4

Whenever an Elder yields up the ghost in Ipepe or anyone of the dwelling places in Atlantic Yoruba, there are many things to be made cryptic to a youth, especially when that youth is yet to be initiated—yet to be shown a book of knowledge. One aspect of a phenomenon to be made glaring to him or her is the act of weeping. Many members of our family wept for days. Their eyes were reddish. Their hairs looked terrible—disheveled. Their teeth saw no chew sticks. Their lips touched no food except chants that recalled the heroic deeds of the deceased and the pride of her long pedigrees. And their eyes beheld nothing, bore nothing but rivulets of tears that portrayed some kind of immortality. The entire family house was interred under the avalanche of sorrow. Faces were long and lugubrious and every spoken word was indicative of mourning—reviling mortality in strong terms. I had some water in my eyes but this was a modicum compared to the weepers' eyes whose lower lids carried something like stalactites. At worst, I would cry myself to sleep. At best, I would be scared, thinking the ancestors might want to show up or spank me for being curious and contumacious.

THE CONFLICT: The death of my grandmother brought a steamy conflict between her father's house and her mother's house. Paternal house versus maternal house, it was. Each house wanted her remains to be buried in its place. While her father's house wanted her remains to be buried in Ugbo or Mahin, her mother's house wanted it to be buried in Agerige, a market town which I had visited on several market days and where I had learnt the art of carrying a small-size bag of gari on my head—balancing it with the confidence and daring characteristic of an acrobat. After many days of hot arguments, her mother's house won. And the ancient woman was laid to rest in the market town of Agerige, about four miles (by trekking) from Zion-Ipepe. The uproarious diatribe, or shall I say disagreement was put to rest and the future of both the paternal and the maternal households is reconstructed again—peacefully and prayerfully.

5

During the burial rituals of the ancient woman, I had the opportunity for the first time in my life to watch the ancestral masqueraders, most of who had bivouacked in an exclusive part of the market town. Some of them would appear as amazing dancers, moving their hips like roulettes, while some would entertain us as amateurish dancers and racers. Because I was not initiated at that time, there were many ritual rites and ceremonies that the Elders forbade me to attend. But lucky was I to be able to burrow into the mysterious but picturesque and heart-moving display of the ancestors including my grandmother who appeared weak and crestfallen for leaving the world, this sorrow-filled world behind her.

On the seventh and the last day of the ritualistic ceremony, during the highs and the lows of the day, I watched a number of the Elders being inducted into the Ancestral Shrine of Immortality. What I experienced for those seven days, I cannot forget a single moment of it till the end of time.

I could not boast much about how I used to carry a load on my head. I was not good at this to be honest. Many times, I was too afraid to put any of those heavy bags of gari on my head. I couldn't remember how many market days I did refuse to carry my own bag of gari. I would try to run away but my good mother would hold me back, saying I should carry my bag—willy-nilly, inasmuch as I would not *eat my fingers* on getting home. Still refusing to obey, my mother would give me a hot-pepper-like spanking. The upshot, I would proceed to cry and sob. Crying and sobbing, I could: it did not matter to my mum as long as I carried the food, needed at home so that I would not resort to *munching my fingers*. It was not a laughing matter to trek a distance of four miles, and balancing a heavy load upon the head.

One foggy morning, when the rays of the sun could hardly reach the earth below, as I woke up from bed, I found my neck stiff and lightly paining me. I could hardly turn it from right to left and vice-versa. During the gloaming, just before the chicks started to roost, a neighbor jocularly said, "Are you the one eating the food, or is it the food eating you?" I did not understand what the joke meant. But on looking at my neck in the mirror, I realized what the joke meant—my head was sinking inside my neck. I had given my head too much work to do. This gave me an open-air reason not to go with my mum to the next market which used to fall on every eight days. A respite in the nick of time.

There was a time, a time I was carrying a pendulum of immortality around my neck. I could not complain or explain why I did fall in love with immortality. I find myself—always like the wind that whistles, breathes and caresses my visage whenever I wake up in the morn and look toward the sky and the flirting cirrocumuli, cirrostrati and cirri –moving back and forth around the sun (as though they want to strangle the sun) like the pendulum of immortality around my neck and the asphodel around my waist.

Everywhere and everything was beautiful, simple, serene and naked with eternity. What a wonderful world as I was growing up? Falling down, bruising my kneecaps, toes and fingers, it was part of immortality. If I misbehaved to my senior and a clout or a glancing slap became my comeuppance, it was part of immortality, so I always thought. There seemed not to be any pain even if I wept and sought the cool embrace of my mother. Sometimes, I felt no hunger—playing football with my age-group friends—from sunup till sundown. Or swimming and diving for hours until our bodies turned green from the green debris in the water, and our eyes turning red like the eyes of a drowning chimp. Life was simply as sweet as the honey whose art of production my father had mastered before I was born. Life was a sweet dream of continuity. I was lucky—still lucky that I was born: born by those who had mothered and fathered me. They are kind to me, through thick and thin. And I don't know how to requite their kindnesses.

Is nature to blame? Yes and no. However, if nature were anything I could taste as I used to taste every nourishing necessaries provided by my parents, I could have tasted the raindrops whose plunking on the water was like a festival of drums—naturally producing rhythms, harmonies and melodies. Running about in the rain—naked, singing rain-songs, and asking God to send more rain for my rubbery skin, is another reason why the joy of the rainy season which I recognize as the dew of youth, will forever be fresh in my memory. The only menaces that often make me to fly high in the firmament and land myself in the arms of the angels are the jiggers, the mosquitoes, the lies, and once in a while, the leeches. Even these menaces are insignificant with the feeling of immortality in me and around me. I can confidently say that the lies are hard to destroy. But by cleaning and washing regularly the bed-sheets and other clothes in the household, they will be destroyed. Comparatively, let me say that the mosquitoes are harder to destroy. But by applying insecticides in the surroundings, by getting rid of all the water-standing places and by making use of mosquito-nets, fumed with mosquito-powder, they will be routed out. Let me infer that jiggers are the hardest, the most stubborn to destroy. They are all over in the town and in the school campus. They are my nocturnal bugaboos and my diurnal nightmares. Wearing shoes, made of rubber or leather, or barefooted like Jesus Christ, it would not help. They would find their way to attack your toes and suck the hell out of your precious blood. Jesus knows I hate them. That is why I cannot remember how many times I would jay-walk like Charlie Chaplin whenever they attacked my toes, burrowing holes into them and causing me a hell of pain, irritation and suppurating shame. That is why I have no solution as to how to destroy them once and for all. The only time my God-given toes would be free of these elfin nuisances was during holidays when I would have no cause to go to Zion-Ipepe and tread upon the parasite-infested pathways.

Rainy season also is a time of plenty. And there is much joy that goes with that feeling of plenitude. It is a time to sing rain-songs. Even the downpours, the thundering rainstorms and the chilly harmattans have their kind of rain-songs that I used to sing as part of the nature of being a youth. Whenever it downpours for hours, the whole Atlantic area will be filled with water: houses will seem as though they will be swallowed by the water I love very much. Water becomes the sole phenomenon. It is therapeutic—a sight for sore eyes. It is like a toy. It is like food. As a matter of fact, it is food, for nothing can be consummated without water, physically or spiritually.

Yet another cynosure is the cinematic appearance of the rain-flooded rivers and lakes. Gosh, the water, reaching to the inside of the stilt houses, allowing the fishes and crustaceans to swim with sheer abandonment to the thresholds of the seemingly floating houses and occupying them as invited guests sans invitations. Now the boats and canoes will reach almost to the top of the red and white mangroves. If I were the giraffe, I would have no (*wahala*) trouble reaching (out) for the best from the treetops and beat my chest repeatedly for being the king of the reach.

If I could tell you anything, I could tell you something that I was born in nineteen hundred and forty or fifty something-plus (19??) in a house-like fishing boat on the Lagos lagoon. I could tell you that I could not be certain as much as I could until I was raised up to the age of ten. That was the period I began to realize that to account for facts does belong to childhood. During that year in which I was born inside a fishing boat on the Lagos lagoon, stretching to all the littoral town-lets and villages that beautifully populated the Atlantic coast, only one thing was undisputed, and that was the fact that my father helped my mother to deliver me on the floor of his fishing boat, shared by the fish of every description. Inasmuch as I don't know when I was born, it stands to reason that everything I am writing about my birthplace and the date of my birth, is the sum total of everything my parents had told me about the happy event.

Chapter Two

Oshun—My Mother's Midwife

DIVINITY-PHILOSOPHER OSHUN DID IT. I wanted my father to divulge more information on what occurred during my birth. Divinity-Philosopher Oshun, the apple of God's eye, the goddess of love, productivity and watery places gave my father a helping hand! It sounds unbelievable—a cock-and-bull story. Why was it that she did not stop my father from fishing that day so that my mother could deliver me at home as she had been doing to those before me? Was it a mark of honor or dishonor to be born inside a boat—a fishing boat? These are the questions that often bulldoze the asphodels of my days and deracinate the amaranths of my nights whenever I think of the place of my birth.

According to my parents, I was born when the roosters were crowing, when the sun was rising, when the rainbow was making a mark on the western sky with its iridescence, soon after the rain had hit the surface of the earth with its musical sound of a happy event.

Eight days later when it pleases all the deities and the ancestors, under the chapter and verse of Olorun that they should give me names, they named me Arowolo B'Oyinbo. This special name was given to me because I was born at the peak of their fishing industry, epitomizing happiness and success with lots of beans, like a well-to-do white person. I was made to understand beyond quandary that I was the harbinger of the family's wealth. It was no surprise, therefore, that my father had success and wealth—the most successful fisherman among his peers. He could fish when the sea is rough like the body of a shaggy dog. He could fish when the sea is smooth as the face of a newborn. He could fish during a downpour when the raindrops cascading down the cheeks are like the tears shed during the loss of a loved one. During a harmattan season, when visibility would be unbelievably terrifying: so terrifying and poor that it would be blamed on fogging, my best male of a human being, could fish with little or no complaints. (There is one singular exception though. My father could not fish whenever the currents are violently swift and menacing like a whirlwind.) On rivers and lakes, my father's prowess is second to none. Catching of the kings of the seas and oceans— whales, was as easy as catching the tiger sharks. No wonder he was called a marksman who could spear, with one eye closed, a butterfly in its erratic flight. He hardly missed his mark. And I can recall only once when he missed his mark. That was when he took me with him to empty the fish in his fishing traps. On our way home, we saw the king of the freshwater fish arapaima, native to South America, a prize fish, locally known as *agbadagiri*. He waved at me—for silence and focus—as I was endeavoring to control my singultus which often occurs whenever I see a quarry, whetting my appetite. Soon, he began to sharpen the barbed copper point or copper head of the spear and the verdigris came off it in powdery flakes. Then he adjusted the weapon and as the fish came to the surface to inhale, the fisher released his spear. The spear landed on the quarry's abdomen, piercing it through, causing the fish to escape—amazingly. Looking at me at the rear of the boat, my father asked me to restrain my hiccup, assuring me that the fish's head was going into my mother's kedgeree's cooking pot and then to be munched tastefully and lip-bitingly, adding that his spear had been dedicated to Divinity-Philosopher Ogun. Taking his aim, the second time and smiling munificently like an optimist who believed that Divinity-Philosopher Ogun could not let him down, he released his spear with a whistling sound and the dangerous invention landed on the lower jaw of the prize fish. The catadromous fish tried several times to disengage itself but it was too late. Before I started hiccupping—joyfully, the quarry had already been pulled out of the water into the middle hold of the boat with a flop. My father smiled and indicated to me that he had done what makes

12

a fisher a good fisher. Time to go home had arrived. Time to smack my lips and to bite my tongue is just a few hours away. But before smacking my lips, and biting my tongue, I will have to help my mother wash the mortar and the pestle and then pestle the cassava balls and grind the pepper. This is the part every youth plays in the family.

Another remarkable day (remarkable and unforgettable) is a day in the month of December 1958. My father took me to fish with him on Lake Apata, one of the lakes in the vicinity of Ipepe. As always, I was at the rear of the canoe-like punt, paddling. After say, one hour, we had caught some fish—mostly tilapias and mullets.

As we were preparing to go home, my circumspect father spotted a shoal of mullets, racing and springing, one after the other. By the time I paddled the canoe closer to them, they had stopped springing. Presently, they had taken to swimming in a merry-go-round, designed to deceive the piscatorial man. At this juncture, a storm was gathering threat and peril. Fear had succeeded in entering the sinews of my boyhood and my limbs had commenced to tremble. But on remembering the presence of my lion-hearted father, the fear soon packed and departed.

My father tried several times to spear at least one mullet from the shoal but to no avail. Their prowess in racing surprised me and my father was no less astounded. The mullets seemed to have mocked my father's ability to spear without missing.

The last attempt took us to the southern banks of the lake where a lone tree was standing. As my paddle collided accidentally with the tree, I beheld a bee attacking me rather mercilessly for disturbing its peace. It stung my lips and my right ear. "Oh Olodumare, my boy is under attack. Take cover. Take cover, Boyinbo," shrieked my father, and pulled the canoe away from the vicinity of the tree where the bee had built its home. It was too late. The damage had been done. And the fisherman was sorry for his son.

Within minutes, my lips swelled to the size of a pig's snout and my right ear competed roundly, half the size of an elephant's ear. I was in pain for almost a week. It was an excruciating pain. I must say it loud! It was as though sharp nettles were hooked to my lips and my right ear. Ointment was applied to both parts on reaching home but I did not remember how my father managed to extract the venomous stings.

My lips and my right ear, as swollen as they were, did not stop my going out and playing with my friends and acquaintances. Some did not recognize me. A few who recognized me betwixt certainty and uncertainty would ask themselves on approaching them, "Who is this coming like the Boat-Child?"

Since this attack: since this war was waged upon me by this insect of poisonous stings of mass defense, the bees never again attack me or run after me even if I veered into their habitat and rudely provoked the serenity of their privacy. Reason is that my parents have admonished me never to stir, swat or attempt to run away whenever I chance upon them. They have become my friends even if they possess stings of mass destruction!

"Maybe I have bitten them and left my stings still in their abdomens," I said this once to myself—humorously, and with a face wreathed in smiles.

"Don't be funny, Boat Child," said my alter ego, laughing hysterically, cathartically and melodramatically. Again, I heard the voice of my alter ego, "To be a friend of nature is to be a friend of life. If such be the will of the Creator, you will continue to enjoy every ingredient of immortality."

Many times, more than a few times I could repel laziness, I would fail or refuse to wash the plates I used for my meals. I would not listen to my mother even when she would tenderly tell me like this: "Be a good boy, wash what you used to enjoy your meal. Listen to what people are telling you. You're not supposed to be built everyday like a house." But the stubborn boy would not listen like a changeling incarcerated in a cocoon of recalcitrance. All he wanted to do was to join his ululating friends, wrestling or playing football on the wetland field—feeling good at the delirium of debonairness.

14

But my father, the lion of the family would pin me down with his overwhelming authority. "Who do you think is your servant?" he would roar. "You were not asked to cook or perform any other task. All you need to do is to wash the plates—your own plates. And you want to go out with your white man's pointed nose, leaving behind you your responsibility? Is that not so? Supposed you saw the food and you were unable to eat it? Supposed you ate it and you were confronted with the problem of swallowing it? Is there any gumption here to be grateful to your kind-hearted provider, Olodumare? If playing with your friends is the priority, go out and play with them and never you come back home."

A Truncated and Unpropitious Day: My father's anger and semi-disappointment in me could only be compared to that of a wounded lion. (The reason the semi-disappointment did not echo to the cupola is that I was born at the height of the prosperity of the lion's fishing industry. Thus the meaning of my name *Arowolo B'Oyinbo* is an echo of our/his prosperity, spiritual wellness, wealth, success and happiness.) One incident worth mentioning without remembering it was when the stubbornness of my younger brother Ade led to a bovine stupidity. My father asked him to listen to him two times. But he did not stop flirting with his sheer obduracy of wanting to have it his own way. On the third time, my father rose up gingerly, grabbed him by hand and started cudgeling him. After three or four lashes, the fleet-footed cub of a lion bolted away. My father ran after him, ululating and uttering "stopped, stopped." Ade declined to stop. Seeing that he was no match for his own son, my father reached out for the collection of his spears, pulled one out and progressed to aim at him. Scared that he might release the deadly spear, I held to its rear and called for help. Sooner than expected, my mother rushed out from her cubicle. She was bemused and shocked on beholding the spear in the hands of her doting husband. Without much ado, she called the neighbors for help,

15

while praying her loving husband to temper his boiling anger with divine patience.

Meanwhile, Ade who had created some distance betwixt my father and himself, stopped abruptly, looking empty like someone who had been burnt to a frazzle, quivering and burping, retching, crying and sobbing. He was half-scared to death on seeing a weapon of mass-fish-destruction pointing at him, which could have hit him without any trajectory. About five minutes later, Lot, my father's cousin who had heard my mother's call for help arrived on the scene, terrified. While trying to wrench the spear out of my father's hand, he pleaded, "Boda, you don't want to kill your own son even if you have flown into a passion."

On hearing his cousin's voice, my father's boiling anger started to cool down. In his defense, he harrumphed and said, "Lot, he is my son. Anyone of them who fails to heed my words will pay for it."

"B-o-d-a," reposted Lot, drawling out the word, B-o-d-a, "spearing him is not the best way to reprimand or scold him. Neither is it the best way to truncate his recalcitrance."

Still shocked, bemused and looking helpless, and cupping her lips in shilly-shally, my lioness-mother, shook her head left and right. Then staring at her doting husband and releasing an infectious, pretty-good pout in an inauspicious day said in a mother-is-good voice, "I never can understand your mind. But I am not nonplused, for one must be a creature of all seasons to understand the vagaries of human emotions."

Consequently, some flimsy smile of understanding and forgiveness began to open the tight corner of my father's lips. Out of discomfiture and fright, a happy spirit commenced to befriend me, on sensing that the matter had been put to half-rest, defying a flash in the pan, after the cub had shown some remorse, a remorse indicating to the lion that he, the cub, would invariably cut his coat according to his size henceforth, learning how to mind his p's and q's. Ever since that day, I have determined more than ever to treat my parents' words with deference.

As for Ade, he was not the same for more than five days, for he suffered the pangs and stings of recalcitrance and disrespect. Slowly but steadily, and with the help of a full-fledged forgiveness on the countenance of the lion, he was healed completely. The family heaved a sigh of relief as the matter is put to rest—diametrically. Since that day, he tried not to allow his dyed-in-the-wool attitude grow beyond roundedness to a form or shape known as a square.

How Father Lion (builder of houses and boats) and Mother Lioness smiled, laughed, cachinnated, poked jokes over the matter: kissed, caressed and settled the matter loving-wisely under their floral mosquito net was/is none of my business. It was a domain beyond the compass of my comprehension in the years of semi--innocence. Even now.

I would obey and suffer in silence my father's raillery about my pointed nose, the most pointed and European-like nose in the family. Having an occidental nose without being born in the Occident is a mystery but good omen to the family who always expects surprises from heaven above. Sometimes I would stand before the mirror and examine for minutes the pointedness of my nose. I would hold it between my thumb and my index finger—swinging it up and down, left and right. Alas, I could not find out how it was so different from the noses of my siblings. However, it was, and indeed it has always been the target regarded as the weakest point of my body, created in the image and the likeness of my heavenly Father—whenever my family members (including friends and the nodding acquaintances) wanted to ridicule me or simply wanted to compare my physiognomy with theirs.

If there is anything to remember, let me remember how onerous it was to scale those fishes—about two thousand sometimes. In some cases I would (like other siblings) not be allowed to eat until the scaling was done. More often than not, I would call upon some of my friends to give me a helping hand.

17

In many instances, my body would be covered with scales. And whenever that happened, my loving mother or anyone of my elder sisters would jocularly say that I had nearly turned myself into tilapia, adding that I would need buckets of water and bars of soaps in order to scour myself clean. My good mum is enamored to such a joke and I have inured myself to it. I can't have enough words to describe those piscatorial experiences. Those experiences are wonderful and equally memorable. And the tilapia and their eggs—the hard roe—oh God of the littoral dwellings—are so palatable and mouth-watering, whenever baked, roasted or cooked. Munching a tilapia, especially *ekikin*, a family of tilapia, a rarity, often difficult to catch, is like munching manna, released directly from the Holy Spirit's kitchen of comestibles.

Low and behold: "Going to school is boring." This pronouncement was common on the lips of those youths who have fallen head over heels in love with fishing, and who have placed their well being on the palatability of tilapias or *ekikin*. Sometimes I would joyfully ask myself whether eating good is synonymous to immortality via good health.

Most of the tilapias are caught when the dry season is approaching and soon after. The delicious white marine crayfish, and the yabbies, the less delicious small freshwater crayfish, are found during this period of the year, also.

Prior to his retirement and the time he was made a Chief, many fisher-men-to-be came from other littoral villages seeking his advice, knowledge and experience of fishing. Many were surprised to learn that he taught them nothing except these words: "Always ask Divinity-Philosopher Ogun to clear the way for you and Divinity-Philosophers Olokun, Oya and Oshun will bring everything to your hearts' contents."

In all the traits of comprehension, pairing it up with the knowledge that destroys ignorance, I did not realize that my humble father could not tell the world enough how much Creator-Philosopher Olodumare had helped him. This spirit of humility might be as a result of his mild stammering (not as serious as that of Okonkwo in Chinua Achebe's *Things Fall Apart*) whenever he spoke. This might be one of the factors why our family is invariably at peace. Husband and wife had planted seeds of peace and the results were poured upon them like a shower of spiritual wellness. Only one time I saw my father, shrieking, yelling, bawling, growling, barking, and roaring (like a lion) at my mother, "I am not your equal, Matilda. You may be a good fisher like me but you can't dream of catching the prize fish let alone the biggie of the seas and oceans. I can be smooth. I can be rough. I can be soft. I can be tough. But I am not your equal and all the orisas can attest to this."

Like a lioness, my mother's reply was simple, feminine and affectionate. It was affectionate to the degree of releasing an infectious and spell-binding smile, for she knew that the lion was just bragging about his leonine machismo. She knew that his bark could be worse than his bite, sometimes. There was an interlude of silence, in which I found myself. Whenever maternal and paternal affection conflicted, I was invariably in the middle to revel in the sound of silence as produced by reason. Sooner than expected, the interlude of silence was broken by adorable words from my father who appeared to be supple like a kitten. As my stomach was trembling with delectation, the good-for-something feeling overwhelming me is that I was pleasantly and dramatically entertained. Here is a lion of a man: a best-selling fisherman who came from his father's homeland in Ode-Omi because of the lioness. Here is a man who was *dying to marrying* my mother (according to his own confession) because of my mother's gorgeous hair cascading upon her shoulders, fanning her face whenever the weather became breezy. Others signs of physical beauty why he married my sweet and smooth-speaking mother are: white teeth, narrow ankles, small-caressing fingers, slopping shoulders, broad pelvis, thin and smooth forearms, and a slender neck, garlanded with little folds of flesh.

My mother also was a bestselling fisher in her own right. Like my father, she was able to catch catadromous and anadromous fishes. If she had to write a book on her piscatorial career, she could easily become a bestselling author. She is good but my father always shows her that he is her husband, a man, and the breadwinner whose machismo cannot be mistaken for femininity.

These blessed experiences did not come directly from the Providence but from Oshun, the undisputed goddess of productivity, love, wealth and peace. Looking back today, I feel like telling Divinity-Philosopher Oshun: "You are the seer of rivers, you live among the smooth-flowing currents and rhythms of rivers where your force moves ever forward. Around your neck are the petals of asphodels and amaranths. You are the adorer of exquisite trinkets and wear-me-rich clothes. You are a passion-dancer and the bearer of sweet love. You are divine. You are a charmed comforter. Your bearing of fierce temperament cannot be compared to your milk of divine kindness. You are one of the Bringers of Light and Creative Energy. You are the cool water that brings panacea to the abdomen and the children to the barren. I feel like—certainly not forced of asking you why your faculty as a Divinity-Philosopher of muliebrity allowed my mother to deliver me inside a fishing boat—like a feral child? Will the world regard this a slap on my face or on my back? How will your insouciant attitude prevent people from calling me a weirdo, a boat-child, a wonder-boy? Who is going to issue me a peremptory note to plead my cause?

Chapter Three

Bed and Back Wetting

People may refer to me as a weirdo, a boat-child or a wonder-boy but there is another eye-brow raising phenomenon that happened to me as I was going through the formative years of my life. If anyone does refer to me using the above-named words, such a reference might come from people who never bed-wetted.

How can I describe the situation? All I know was that the situation was disgusting, dirty, irritable, nasty, terrible, appalling, tempestuous, lamentable, annoying and painful. What I thought I could do to alleviate this self-inflicted pain was a possibility that my mind could not distantly conjecture. The painful situation which I am referring to is about bed wetting in which I was a huge concern to my mother. I wetted her bed in general and my bed in particular, almost every night—giving my body and my bed a nose-twisting smell that could be compared only to sulphuric halitosis. It was as though all my dreams were dreams of how to wet a bed. It was as though all the urine in my urinary bladder was meant for my bed. It was as if Oshun, Olokun and Oya, the deities dealing with fluidity were not happy with me. This is a speculation. The three deities have no reason to be unhappy with me. After all, one of them, Oshun is the one that helped my mother to deliver me.

Wetting my bed everyday and every night was not one of the beautiful experiences that used to put smiles on my mother's lips. My mother used to be upset, especially when she thought I should have made wetting history. The actual age when I stopped wetting my bed is not known. Certainly, I did not stop embarrassing my mother until I was four or five rainy seasons.

It was not only my bed that used to have a puddle of pee but also my mother's back was a victim. Also containing puddles of urine was my mother's valuable gazar which she used to tie me securely to her back. A gazar is a piece of silk or cotton material of loose making with a stiff hand. It is like a mother's cummerbund. As with every mother of love, my mother would carry me on her back for a jiffy, say two or three minutes. And in another jiffy of a time, I would start wetting her back. This is the most annoying part of back wetting. Whenever this happened, my mother would start talking to me like this, "Careless kid, what are you doing? Why did you do this to me? Why didn't you pee before asking me to carry you?" She would put me down and give me some "academic spanking," designed to teach me how to conduct myself. Alas, many of her spankings did not stop me from wetting. Poor hoodoo, I could not say with certitude that I was undergoing some kind of pain which I could swap for a futuristic advantage, for any creation to have a meaningful existence in life, it must experience some form of corporeal pain, even spiritual.

As far as my memory could carry me, and as good as I can remember, everyone of my male siblings had this problem of bed and back wetting. There seemed to be no remedy for it. But some parents did say that there is a solution to bed wetting by asking the bed-wetter to piss on live charcoals every time the bed-wetter wanted to sleep. My parents did not ask me to do this in spite of my bed and back wetting. Why they did not ask me to piss on live charcoals was/is not clear to me till today. I guess they wanted the situation to take its natural course: its natural course?! Who says it is natural in my life that is flooded with tapestries? Nine months of carrying me in her stomach plus three to four years of wetting her back and bed: o mother and mothers, how could you all have borne these ugly situations with love-emblazoned complaints and spankings tempered with passion if not because of your unsurpassable love for me and other children who have badly carried themselves like me, in their formative years of beauty, love and tenderness? I may go on and on with hundreds of rhetorical questions, nothing will change. For my words, as for my unspoken words, no one is present today to change anything or to answer anyone of them.

Chapter Four

You Will Be a Bringer of Light

"You will be a bringer of light. A bringer of light, you will become. You will be a bringer of light as well as a keeper of traditions and a learner of the Book of Enlightenment. Your days will be spent with thrills of joys and your nights will be inundated with dreams that will surprise you as you reminisce about life and death. You will remain a bringer of light as long as there is the earth to tread upon, air to breathe in and out, and water to drink. You are a bringer of light and this may explain why you will be an object of jealousy amongst your many detractors, some of whom are taking leave of their senses. But no matter their numerical strength or power, they can do no insidious harm to your spirit, for no one is angry with the earth without treading upon it, for no one is angry with the air without breathing it in and out, for no one is angry with the water without drinking it. Keep honoring your parents and your Elders and do not allow the grass to grow under your feet when it comes to punctuality."

The foregoing is what the divination says of me as I was growing to become a termite of a lad. But I had no knowledge of this until years later, when I was relishing the fruits of adolescence. In Yoruba-land, prior to the adulteration of its traditions, consulting the Book of Enlightenment, otherwise known as the Ifa-Ife Board of Divination, is very imperative after the birth of a child. In many cases, the consultation continues as long as the child lives. It is a joyful phenomenon.

As I was treading upon the earth, breathing in and out the impalpable air, drinking water more and more into my system, I was made to understand that head (ori) is the most important part of human body—the taproot of our existence: that whatever is ailing the head will metastasize to the rest of the

25

body. Thus during the years of my innocence, the diviners, sometimes called the prophets of the land or the bucolic philosophers, endowed with various gifts, as well as the gift of the gab, in cooperation with my parents, would make sure that I possess a worthy life (an old head on young shoulders) in which I should be growing with abundant happiness.

Those *mysterious* people, in mysterious and voluminous garbs, often referred to as the keepers of traditions and the mouth-pieces of the deities, and who are very wary of their long pedigrees, would let me know that the Yoruba people are the scions of Oduduwa, the heroic king, the primogenitor and the founder of the ancient, holy city of Ile-Ife, and because every son and daughter of the land belongs to the Oduduwa dynasty, every son and every daughter could be called a prince and a princess, respectively. I did not think a whit in a moment that I would one day become a king. What I know and adore is immortality, emblazoned with happiness, derived/emanating from the contradictions of nature.

Chapter Five

Ipepe, the Miracle Town-let

Giving birth to babies is the first song a married woman knows how to sing in Ipepe, one of the littoral town-lets, lying southeast of Lagos and its lagoon. I grew to know that only a few women had money in the fifties but they had children. Having children is like having money—even more than money in some families. Generally, and indeed with some rain of blessings, those who had many children and a lot of money were extremely lucky. They are the women whose supplications had been answered by Creator-Philosopher Olodumare via the ancestors and other benevolent deities, especially Divinity-Philosopher Oshun, the goddess of productivity, who is presently called the advocate for women's human rights. She must have inspired Queen Funmilayo Kuti in her philosophy to stand up for women's rights in the thirties, forties, fifties and sixties.

What is interesting about Ipepe which can as well be funny is that it has its houses hanged in the air—and the water staying still or flowing beneath the houses depending on the temperament of Divinity-Philosopher Oshun. In other words, every house in Ipepe is built on stilts. During the rainy season, canoes, boats feluccas, and wherries are the means of transportation. When the dry season comes and the sun begins to siphon the water, walking (on what looks like a wetland) becomes the mode by which people move from one place to another.

Ipepe was growing as I was growing up as an un-licked boy—grasping the awareness of my surroundings. That was immediately after my initiation and shortly before I broke my voice. The town-let was growing in an unusual way that one could not compare with Lagos. The only usual way I can think about is that the two places are on the lagoon and can mercilessly be wiped out of the surface of the earth by a monster tornado if not for the grace of the Supreme Being. But it is certain and often thought to be inaccurate the widespread news that the cathedral city of Lagos and other littoral homes had struck a spiritual deal with Divinity-Philosophers Oya, Olokun and Oshun to shield them from the wrath of impending tornadoes or any natural calamities that might bring blood and sorrows to the hearts of their citizens.

As I was increasingly aware of myself and the world surrounding me, I saw my father one afternoon in the company of his age-group friends offering a votive sacrifice (a dog) to Creator-Philosopher Olodumare through Divinity-Philosopher Ogun, the artificer and the Commander-in-Chief of iron and steel. After the immolation, I asked my father with some trepidation and uncertainty in my voice why he and his colleagues were still worshipping the Creator through Ogun. His answer, simple and reflective: "Boy, before the Bible came to our threshold, we never forget worshipping the Creator through our deities. Not quite three months ago, our clergyman said that the Satan or Devil tested Jesus Christ to the point of committing a debt of failure before God. Jesus, we are told, is undeniably the Son of God, Olorun Oba. If the Satan could shake Jesus Christ with temptations, who are we, or how could we defend ourselves on a daily basis without being tormented by the fearful Satan and his witchy assistants/collaborators and followers?" I left my father's presence armed with the belief that there is nothing dying in worshipping Creator-Philosopher Olodumare through his creatures.

A few months later, I stood by the bank of a lake and prayed Divinity-Philosophers Oshun, Oya and Olokun to always protect me while drinking water, while under a downpour, while fishing, while swimming and while paddling my canoe and rowing my boat. I asked the three of them to protect me from the diabolic Satan and his wicked contemporaries.

The following day, I took in my hand the family's cutlass and adjured demythologized Ogun to protect me whenever I use it. I asked him to use it to clear the road for me while going to fetch water, while going to fetch firewood, while going to fish, while going to hunt quarries. I asked the inventor and the commander-in-chief of steel and iron to be my personal security guard who will be ready at anytime to cut into two the Satan or anyone of his mercenaries. Divinity-Philosopher Ogun has vowed, apparently to do this with the permission of the Author of Life and Death.

Socially, Ipepe is a place where songs and roundelays can be heard at anytime of the day by the women who had turned their kitchens and boudoirs into rendezvous. There are groups of women whose traditional styles of braiding often whet men's appetites. By the end of every year, there are problem plays— helping the youth to acquire old heads on their young shoulders. The sublimity or shall I say tranquility of the town-lets often forces one to slumber when least expected. Here every Elder schools himself/herself to become a keeper of every youth. Conversely, every youth is a humble son or a daughter of an Elder.

Ipepe has one weakness, weaker than Achilles' heel. I cannot continue laughing, singing and dancing without mentioning it. This weakness blemishes our hard-working women who did not like to stay in their husbands' matrimonial homes on being given to marriage. In the past, many would run back to Ipepe with tears in their eyes telling how heavy-handed their husbands were. Whenever a wife accused her husband of brutality which is another word I am using for heavy-handedness, the husband would be summoned to a family meeting. The husband would tell his own side of the story. The woman would tell her own version of the story—usually and not always with tears of suffering in her eyes.

During the hour of judgment, the father-in-law would raise his voice say like this, "I so and so advise you to try everything under the sky to make your wife a happy woman. This is what you own her, not fighting or brutality."

The mother-in-law would pout and re-pout and then say something like this, "This is my only daughter, carried inside my stomach for nine lunar moons, and on my back for six months. It is your duty to learn how to treat her with unsurpassable affection. Remember she needs you as you need her. Running away from you because of your heavy-handedness, is not her dream of marrying you. Nor is it my dream of allowing you to marry her. My beautiful daughter needs nothing but your love. Let her feel it from head to toe. This is her cure-all: her panacea."

If the son-in-law is found guilty, he will pay for his heavy-handedness after he must have asked for forgiveness— promising that he would never again hit his wife. A fine of wine or a goat or both was a commonplace.

The son-in-law will now be awaiting the arrival of his beloved wife in his house. After waiting for two or three weeks, without his wife in sight, he will pack his belongings and leave for Ipepe—adding a number to its ever-growing population. This is how the population of Ipepe has been growing with men from other town-lets and villages.

There is one particular man, a one-man band musician who said that Ipepe is like a paradise to him after staying in the town-let for one year. The music-man came from a littoral town-let whose name I have forgotten. It is relatively far but not too far for those who like to row or paddle.

What made "Melody Man" (as he is adorably and musically being addressed) call Ipepe a paradise is the reason and the sensibility why he fell head over heels in love with a woman of his dreams. The woman treated him like a prince and he treated the woman like a princess. Things went peacefully and smoothly for both of them. Happiness becomes their portion. After six moons of courtship, he married his sweetheart.

In one of his lyrics, Melody Man admitted that he had found his luck, his gold, diamond and honey in a woman and would never ever go back to his birthplace. This charismatic man is the first one-man band semi-professional musician I have the opportunity to know. He plays guitar and accordion artistically and his songs are ever romantic and heart-felt. He is the talk of the town—musically. The joke about him is that he has been hooked and enchanted by the sweetness between the thighs of a goddess.

This song I remember of him:
I came like a tourist
I am staying like a citizen
Life could be sweeter beyond one's birthplace
Here in Ipepe I've found a new life.
Sweet, sweet life with my sweet-heart.

That Melody Man's presence did add an extra spice from the ritualistic grains of paradise to the musical life vis-à-vis atmosphere of Ipepe cannot be disputed. I count myself fortunate to have watched him play several times.

Why many people like to settle in Ipepe, apart from those who were lured by their wives, are not very clear till this moment of reasoning. Some rumors had it that it was because its citizens are brave, resourceful, smart and fist-happy. But some distant rumors gathered by professional eavesdroppers speculated that it is because of its geographical location (its proximity to Lagos, definitely an advantage), its classical and miraculous stone house of worship—on the middle of a lake, and its openness to modern education—giving birth to a Primary School and a Junior High School.

Today, things have changed, for the beautiful daughters of Ipepe have learned how to love, marry and stay in their matrimonial homes until death separate them from their proud and lucky husbands.

Every other year, the Ipepe Social Club holds a festival. About six months before it begins, the public relations officer will start bruiting about the news that the festival will take place on a set date. Rehearsals will be held so as to avoid any flop. All

31

the members of the club will be up and doing. The par for the course will be maintained.

On the very day of the festival, a boat will lavishly be decorated. Consequently, the leader (otherwise called the captain) and other members of the club will board the decorated boat and go from one part of the town-let to another—singing, clapping, dancing and indicating to the world that they are ready to paint the world the color of a rainbow and to fill the ether with a brand new cloud of entertainment.

After, say two hours of parading, the decorated boat will be moored to the parade ground—always the compound of Chief Olatuga. The parade ground is always fenced with banners, cloths and palm-fronds. Here they will commence to wear their festival uniforms—colorful and always a sight for the sore eyes. And always must be judged to be better than the previous festival uniforms, especially when other clubs are involved or invited. The highlights of the festival will be visible when the singing starts and the drums begin to sound, inducing the neck-powdered female members to rise to the center of the stage, rolling their bums and waltzing their shanks—sending a tempest-like intoxication into the secret recesses of the male members. The festival usually lasts five to seven days and each day has a program different from the other.

My next of kin, Eliam Omojuwa and I had attended Ipepe Social Club many times. Sometimes we would dance when the drums started to sound and the songs started to sink into our skins and marrows. Apart from the fact that most of its members are professional fishers, the Ipepe Social Club, an entertainment club, teaches the Ipepe youths the values of a non-for-profit organization.

While most of the female youths find their niche in Ipepe Social Club, most of the male youths find their niche in Ipepe Student Association. Founded as early as 1958, the Ipepe Student Association in which I was once a secretary was very active before it became moribund when most of the youths in

Ipepe and Zion started milling to Lagos in search of white-collar jobs.

At the end of every year, the association would hold a concert-party in which dramas or play-lets would be performed to the gusto of invitees—mostly our sisters, brothers, mothers and fathers.

Its mission is to promote unity among the Ipepe sons and daughters scattered all over the country, asking them to contribute to the development of the miracle town-let. Thus reminding them not to forget their ancestral homeland wherever they might reside.

Culturally, stories, especially morality stories, usually conflated with fairytales in which Ijapa, the prestidigitator, often depicted as a tortoise representing the rhythms, the harmonies and the melodies of the Yoruba act of storytelling, enlivens every heart, young and old, especially during a crescent-lit night. Wrestling and the game of ayo, and hide and seek, coupled with playing possums are common. Also, playing dove is common during dry seasons. Dove is a crude kind of golf. Holes are made in the shape of a dove on the ground and players at a marked distance on the ground will take turns to roll a ball into one of the holes. Whosoever rolls the highest number of balls into the holes will be declared a winner—winning the applause of the onlookers. Other littoral town-lets and villages often refer to Ipepe and Zion-Ipepe as a cultural oasis, a fountainhead of the world of ideas.

Economically, Ipepe is a leader among other littoral dwelling places that produce sea-foods. Most of its sea-foods can be found in the kitchens, and on the tables, as far away as Kano. It prides itself as the sole town-let that successfully understands how to hunt whales. It is one of the few places where their men and women are regarded, and indeed with kudos, as hard-working machines of human beings.

Politically, this miracle town-let has nothing to write home about. It is apolitical. The political vortexes in Lagos and Ibadan did not spill to the ears of its citizens. Nor their bickering heard below the vault of heaven.

Religiously, the town-let is a spiritual haven which knew no Christians or Muslims at the time I was growing up as unlicked lad. Concoctions and medicinal vials to ward off evil spirits and witchy workers of nightmares were common. Sacrificing dogs and chicks to gods and goddesses were rife: sometimes on a weekly basis. Sacrifices offered in the evening usually disappeared before dawn. Sooner than later, it occurred to me that Ijapa who is often depicted as a tortoise, is a stunt human being, a prestidigitator, a messenger of Creator-Philosopher Olodumare—between heaven and earth—carrying votive (evening and night) oblations to the Supreme Being, before dawn.

Soon after Ipepe stumbled into the orbit of the missionaries from the Christian Missionary Society of the Church of England (CMS), a brick church perches miraculously, almost majestically upon a muddy panhandle of the town-let. It is the first "floating church" of its kind (of bricks and mortars) in all the town-lets and villages encircled by the lagoon. The actual year of its erection and the providers of the cement used to build it, remains a mystery till today. That sense of mystery has always energized the people of Ipepe that they have the unbelievable faith in the mysterious Creator of heaven and earth to do anything they want to do with the help of the Creator and his messengers. Referring to that faith in God as a fulfillment rather than the gift of the gab, their sense of mystery is justified whenever they refer to a church whose date of erection and its builders are unknown and a boat boy—a wonder boy whose birthday is unknown to him, to anyone except his parents. If there is anything that will be something that I will remember till the end of time about the floating brick church, that something is the bronze bell of its belfry. Occasionally, I took part in tolling the bell, summoning the Sunday congregation.

Generally, the rainy and dry the seasons tell the characters of Ipepe and other town-lets and villages of the Atlantic. The significance of the rainy season is that there is an abundance of water to use and much more. Oh the jinnee of the rainy season, you are so awesome and body and spirit refreshing with your therapeutic pitter-patter. The lakes and rivers are full of water. And in the day time, it is very interesting and eyeful to see the breeze blowing ripples of smiles upon them. The trees are luxuriant, especially the red and the white mangroves whose aerial roots are like a mythical sight for sore eyes.

The rainy season, I must add is always boring and makes me and my age-group friends always inactive. During the rainy season, I often resorted to playing ball in my father's sitting room. A few of my friends would happily join me. Some would show up by invitation, some by agreement. We would push to the corner of the sitting room all the furniture, and playing football would commence in earnest. We would play for hours, smashing the ball against the doors and the windows. We would not stop until we heard or saw my father mooring his fishing boat. In a blitz, we would orderly arrange all the pieces of the furniture, conducting ourselves thereafter like good-for-something children. We would comport and compare ourselves to well-behaved boys who would in the future bring honor and credit to the community. More often that not, we played possum. We pretended a lot—hoodwinking ourselves whenever we thought the lion of the house had been deceived. If we broke anything (this occurred whenever luck was at loggerheads with us) or if the neighbor reported to the lion of the house that he/she had been disturbed by a hell of noise during his absence, I would be rebuked scathingly and the piscatorial man would refer to me as a good-for-nothing lad. My friends would also share the same degrading fate. Whenever I found myself wanting in this manner, I would let my head droop in a botanical shame like a child who had stolen its own belonging.

The dry season on the other hand, is a period whose significance is like the opposite of the significance provided by the rainy season. During the dry season, one hardly needs a boat or a canoe to move from one place to the other. The wetland would be leached so much that a burgundy layer would appear on the surface. The compound of the picturesque church becomes a playground for many youths. The awe-inspiring eki-trees whose fire-leaves light the sky, heralding the dry season and the Christmas are noteworthy as they are noticeable. But water supply is scare. Usually if not always, I had to go far away from home before I could fetch two or three buckets or pots of water. Most of the waters of the brooks and lakes have become to roil and spume and saline. I remember water being rationed among my brothers and sisters. Indeed, lack of water, and especially rainwater, during the dry season, is invariably a harbinger of a hard time, as the crowing of the cock in a broad daylight is a harbinger of a hard time.

Chapter Six

The School Days—I

Going to school in the fifties had a lot to do with the headmaster and the parents sitting down and fleshing out the nitty-gritty, the advantages and disadvantages of education in the family. For an able-bodied male youth to leave his father's trade or occupation, and starts going to school, is always secondary in the sight of his father, even his mother. Questions such as these were a commonplace: What can I do alone on the farm without my children? Is it not true that Creator-Philosopher Olodumare has given me these children in order to help me? Is education going to make the family richer? Who will be doing the buying and selling for me in the market if I should allow the teachers to take away my children in the name of schooling?

I started school at the age when my right hand was able to touch my left ear, over my head: conversely, when my left hand was able to touch my right ear, over my head. This was the only optical sign or evidence to show that a boy or a girl is old enough: developed enough to start his/her primary school education, cognizant of his/her multiplication table. Arithmetically, it is like this: $1+2+3=6$, divided by $2=3$. Three is half of six. What this means is that half of your daily life belongs to the teachers and the learning of their unavoidable thrashing, while the other half belongs to the household of your parents and their avoidable spanking.

Like most parents, my parents believe that the primary training of a child begins at home, just as charity begins at home. Also, my parents let me know that a well-trained child comprehends that half a word is enough for a wise. Every child is duty-bound to understand the essence and moral value of respecting and honoring his parents.

Ipepe was and still lucky to have a Community Learning Center at the time the miracle church was built. The Community Learning Center was folded up when Zion was founded in 1951. Mount Zion as it is being popularly called by the sons and daughters of the littoral town-lets is a religious paradise. Mount Zion subscribes to the Cherubim and Seraphim Movement of the world. Its founder, Moses Orimolade Tinulase, founded it with the help of the diaphanous holy ghosts. The other three churches founded with the help of the holy diaphanous ghosts are the Church of Aladura, whose founder is Josiah Olunowo Oshitelu. The Christ Apostolic Church was founded by Pastor Ayo Babalola. The Celestial Church of Christ, founded by Pastor Samuel B.J. Oshofa. These are churches whose philosophies are based on new ways of worshipping God with fasting, praising and praying. They came with a new message which is the message of divinity and Holy Spirit and every member seemed to be climbing an imaginary mount to the Pearly Gates. They all believe in faith healing. "Confess your sins and you will be healed," is the slogan. There are prophets among them who speak in tongues and can see the past, the present and the future snares of the Satan and his diabolic comrades. Some of the prophets are real. Some are as false and deceitful as those of Satan and his tongue of wickedness and embers of brutality.

A few of the real prophets and prophetesses did warn my parents not to use in excess those imported pills and tablets whenever I had a headache or stomachache. Those tablets were many. They came mostly from United Kingdom and Germany. None of them had expiration date. Because of this, they could be used after three or five years—as long as they are available. In absence of a medical advice, the warning from the prophets and prophetesses could therefore be regarded as a divine warning or intervention.

How can I better understand the situation surrounding those pills and tablets than the fact that some of them (if not all of them), on swallowing them, sickened me and my siblings? Sometimes I would vomit so much that I would find it difficult

38

to walk—having deflated my stomach with an overmuch effect. Even to this day, such contemptuous and inefficacious drugs could be found almost everywhere in the country.

In spite of the new way of worshipping Olodumare, the Creator-Philosopher of heaven and earth, Divinity-Philosopher Ogun remains the Muse of the family under the auspices of Creator-Philosopher Olorun or Olodumare. His energy cannot be enervated. His main tools are: the anvil which signifies the earth's ability to transform man, the shovel which he uses for digging into the potential. The machete, he uses to clear the forest and for protection. He uses the rake to gather and to smooth the rough areas of the field. He uses the hoe to cultivate the earth's potential. He uses the hammer to shape the faculties. He uses the pick to penetrate the hardened area of the earth.

Ogun, even if he remains the Muse of the family, was dethroned from the altar of traditional worship to the chagrin of other deities in Yoruba pantheon and replaced by a mighty BIBLE that I could hardly lift up from the escritoire.

His praises are often sung while embarking on a task, for his passé-partout unlocks any place or door which is locked.

Ogun onire ni nje aja
Ogun ikola, a je igbin
Ogun gbena-gbena, oje igi lo nje
O pa sile, o pa soko
Laka aiye Ogun ko laso
Mariwo laso Ogun
Ire ki ise ile Ogun
Emu lo ya mu nibe.

Ogun the owner of Ire
Ogun of circumcision eats snails
Ogun of carvers, saps the juice of trees
He kills in the house, he kills on the farm
He who covers the world, Ogun has no cloth
Palm frond is the cloth of Ogun

Ire is not the home of Ogun
He simply stopped there to drink palm wine.

The reason why my parents allowed me to go to school is that Divinity-Philosopher Ogun refused my sacrifice to become a professional fisher like my siblings. I tried all I could to become a fisher but all my efforts were squashed to my chagrin. The demythologized Ogun does not want me to use his invention in catching fish. And I cannot press a charge against Oshun, Olokun and Oya for telling me to stay away from water and never again bother the fish, under their auspices. Thus my primary school education at Zion-Ipepe Primary School, started in earnest in 1954.

In 1955, the free primary school education under the transcendental premiership of Chief Obafemi Awolowo came into effect. This was a thank-you-relief from every student and every parent who believed that the government had to help the communities whose sons and daughters had left their fishing and farming occupations for the classrooms—tilting their heads toward another world of reading, writing—and eventually becoming the community teachers they never had dreamt about. Thus the name, "AWO" started to ring a bell throughout the Western part of Nigeria for being the first African to give the gift of free education to the people he had pledged to serve.

Arithmetic and English were the primary subjects. The secondary subjects are Nature Study, History, Geography, Religion, Yoruba and Drawing. I enjoyed all the subjects save Drawing. I could not draw even the green snake we saw everyday on the playground. I had no knack of drawing. Anytime I tried to draw, the result would be so poor, like an eyesore, that nothing would be admired but crookedness. I did derive some great fun, though, for our arts master who learnt his own drawing by practicing kept encouraging me to practice everyday until the crookedness of my hand turned to semi-crookedness.

Wednesday is always a day of activities. Sports such as football, four by four relays, high jump, long jump, hop-step and jump, pole fault and a hundred meters dash were the areas of my interest. While some of us would be asked to go a-fishing—for the teachers, some would be asked to work on the school-farm or orchard. Yet there were some who would go a-field to fetch willow-canes used to weave baskets and bamboos to make bamboo-beds. Girls, with some gossips on their lips would sit in groups, knitting the best they had been taught to produce. After some three weeks of learning how to weave good baskets that could well be balanced on the heads of our schoolgirls, sisters and mothers, I was regarded one of the best. The smell of the pride of being one of the best followed me from the school campus to the threshold of my parents.

Truancy was common but not encouraged. And whenever it happened, I would blame it on downpours. Going to school either by paddling a canoe or rowing a boat from Ipepe to Zion-Ipepe, (in a distance of about four nautical mile), is perhaps the most dangerous thing a child would experience in any part of the world. And this I went through until1962 when I moved from Ipepe to Zion-Ipepe for my final examinations. Downpours often led to the soaking of my body and books and my truancy was usually if not always justified whenever it made both the twin-towns depressible, uncomfortable and pitiable. And whenever it rained cats and dogs, the school would be closed. Classes were often rained off whenever the footpath and the classrooms were flooded. Whenever I played truant, my fundament would receive a number of hot-pepper-like cudgels. Corporal punishment, said to be one of the physical ways to let obedience ascend into Britain's heaven and quality of education was as common as the daisies on our football field. Corporal punishments made many of the schoolgirls terrified. Some of them stayed away from classes on hearing that the result of their actions would lead to flogging. No one could avoid corporal punishments because there were many mistakes committed which were either regarded as small-eyed stupidities or bag-eyed behaviors.

Like many students, I tried to satisfy my teachers by behaving well. This was like a competition and there were many disappointments and gnawing of teeth. Why? Because many of us could not measure up to the code of morality which was so high and precious, and I feared many times that I would fall under the attack of kamikaze misbehavior.

On many occasions, I would go with my friends to fetch snails, crickets or to lay snares for the quarries or to gather fruits such as the yellow-berries, the green-berries, the blue-berries, the breadfruit, the pineapples, the succulent schizocarps and the delicious passion-fruit, in various sizes and shapes.

One day, I went by myself. By myself, did I go without informing anyone of my friends, one of whom is Eliam Omojuwa, a very close chum who is not only my next of kin but also my kindred spirit. His father was the vicar of the miracle Anglican Church in a miracle town-let of Ipepe.

As I was stealing cautiously into the wood, the perfumes of the hibiscuses and the lemon grass filled my nostrils to the full. My legs were wetted by the lemon grass, glittering with the dew as the sun emerged to salute the entire world with its willy-nilly grin. My head was occasionally absorbed in the thinking that there might be some rebellious and hostile brownies who wanted to accompany me to my destination. I scouted about my vicinity a little bit and having treated myself to some succulent berries and fetched a bundle of willow canes, I sat upon a pollarded mahogany, under a coppice, in a happy hunting ground, watching a redstart singing and preening by the bank of a slow-moving brook. Its mellifluence never made me doze off. As a matter of fact, I dozed off, for I did not know when a hunter came so close to me as though he had an issue with me. Except for my shorts, I was naked like the nature in its pristine purity. And when the rain came, I was made much more naked. Before my very eyes, I saw a snake gliding across the brook. I saw an ant chasing an ant. I saw a lizard mating. I saw a bee sucking nectar from a hibiscus. I saw a larva metamorphosing into an indigo. I came to the conclusion that nature is

42

beautiful—that the beauty of the world lies in the wholesomeness of the nature—always taking its course. Is this not the way God has ordained the universe? I saw that every creature has its distinct characteristic, ideal for its existence. O nature, how can I purify myself and be a part of your purity.

On one or two occasions, we met oil prospects, *bombing* the vicinity of the school soil, in an optical and aggressive search for petroleum which they had suspected the country has in abundance. One day, as my father heard the dinning sound of the *bombing,* he asked: "Are the occupiers fighting with the freedom fighters again? Is independence still a dream to come true? Or why are they *bombing* and making all those put-putting sounds?"

I replied by saying, "No father, the bombers are bombing the earth into submission. It's a kind of magic submission that will determine the presence of oil in Atlantic Yoruba. Chief Awolowo must have sent them here so that when the oil is discovered, every schoolchild will benefit from it."

As far as I can tell, no oil was found in the vicinity of the school compound save some pieces of terracotta, some of which were used to decorate the flowerbeds.

How lucky is this visionary of a man who believed till he died that the work of a good leader always yields something positive—cocoa production is booming and now oil is being discovered—and so there is enough money for free education for everybody throughout the country.

Chapter Seven

Into the Flames

My father did not know that there were some witchy workers of nightmares watching him and waging a self-destructive war against him. This was a war without a casus belli except that my father was a successful fisher through the grace of Creator-Philosopher Olorun. Must a man be punished because he succeeds through the sheer propensity of hard work?

In 1956, when least expected, my parents got the shock of their lives. My father's house as well as my mother's was burnt down to ashes. It was before my very eyes when the roof and the walls of each house were razed down one by one, turning the whole sky into fireworks. I could not do anything. I was diametrically diffident. I could not even rescue my elder brother's fishing net hung on the frontal beam of my father's house. The conflagration had disoriented me and turned my boyhood into cowardice. I was lucky to be picked up by a neighbor ere the master of the hearth could destroy me: minutes before the roof began to crash and tumble over my head. I was lucky indeed. But my books in a portmanteau were not so lucky. The portmanteau was badly charred and the exercise books inside it looked pitiable. As I started to go through my books one by one, I could hear a crisp sound like a catalytic cracker. Helpless and not knowing what to do with a fire that was not kind to me, I cried and sobbed and sometimes puled like a teacher for what I could not control like a pupil. My brand new portmanteau is gone.

Destroyed together with my parents' houses were a few other houses including the one from which the fire originated. The thingamabob-neighbor whose house started the fire looked as though she had found herself on tenterhooks. Her remorse was indicative of the fact that she was sorry for what her fire had caused.

My father's house had the fortune to be the biggest of all. They were all gutted to the surface of the water. I was innocent even if I could not save the box of my books and a few belongings, especially my elder brother's fishing net.

Towards the end of 1956, something nasty happened to my index finger that nearly broke down my youthful exuberance. It nearly throbbed and troubled the spiritual wellness of the family. That nasty thing was whitlow which brutally attacked the index of my right hand. The inflammation gave me a lot of excruciating pain and sometimes I would whimper, cry and sob, fearing that it would stop me from writing and from going to school. Also, I feared that it would/could metastasize either my thumb or my middle finger. But my loving parents stood by me always. They were worried whenever the shooting pain prevented me from sleeping. My brothers and sisters did not fail to support me too. My teachers as well as my classmates and friends, all supported me and wished me quick recovery. At long last, my parents succeeded in curing the "victim" by means of a native medicinal application—after six lunar months. I am so happy that I can again make use of my indispensable index finger while writing. But my all-purpose index finger remains gangrened till this hour of writing.

Chapter Eight

Taking the Will for the Need

Sympathizers and the downright comforters came from near and far communities to express their deep solicitude for the couple's welfare. They wanted the couple to take the will for the need as the husband and wife found themselves in the desert of dramatic irony. Father and mother looked worried, crestfallen but thankful to Creator-Philosopher Olodumare that even if they lost their belongings, there is no life lost. (Happiness, a lifetime treasure, is more important than the loss of belongings or a collateral damage.) The sympathizers, using verbal nouns and participial adjectives, ruminated over many aspects of life and death. There were elliptical adages, aphorisms and sentences that were unknown to my developing mind—domain of the Elders—the keepers of traditions. Every member of the family was sad and angry. Every member of the family was ill at ease. Even the rainfall was sour with sadness. One sultry evening, my mother perched on her taboret, decked with antimacassar—moaning. My father sat upon his deckchair, decorated with impala skin—pining for the good old days. This tragedy happened barely two years after my father's mother joined the rank and file of the ancestors.

Witnessing an ever-present acronym, *awef*—air, water, earth and fire at such a tender age portends an omen—good or bad, I won't know. But my father, a kind of upstanding gent, invariably standing on ceremony, who believes every child must strive to discover for himself/herself just a little bit of the miracles and secrets of life, always enjoys his silence with tight lips. Here I am, following his footsteps. Hence I was not out of joint to discuss the tragedy and its collateral damage with my school classmates.

Six moons later, my parents' houses were rebuilt—stronger, bigger and more beautiful.

The doors and windows were gabled, like the doors and windows of the miracle church, reminding one of the classical architecture. Friends and acquaintances fell in love with the novel idea. This is like an accretion to the saying in Yorubaland that the rebuilding of a king's palace after it has been burnt, makes it a lot more beautiful.

As would be expected, prophets, rustic philosophers, diviners, including a pythoness started looking for the root of the cause of the conflagration. They found out that the Satan had entered the minds of some people, twisted them upside down and led them to set my parents' houses on a destructive fire, not knowing that they were indirectly destroying themselves in the sight of the Providence. These destructive enemies, most of whom are workers of nightmares, never thought there could be suppurating evidences for what they have done. But there are, for they can only hide. They have nowhere to run into. For if they dare to run, they will end up in the lake of fire—their last abyss of destruction. The wiles of the Devil will certainly be the downfall of the Devil.

Chapter Nine

The School Days—II

Generally, our stern parents were not only drinking gari of happiness but they were also beaming with pride of their children. They, like our strict teachers would never spare their rods whenever we stumbled into a dust bowl of recalcitrance, crassitude and goat-like stubbornness. Sitting on the lap of luxury as initiated by serendipity was a rare indulgence my parents as my teachers would allow for too long. There was no room for hebetude. Things must be done on time and properly too.

Our stern parents as well as our strict teachers always wanted us to look clean in our uniforms. And in order not to run the gauntlet of their sever criticisms, I learned how to wash my clothes by myself. Many times my mother and my sisters helped in washing them for me. To actually look clean, fine and dandy, I learned how to produce iron-lines in my shorts and shirts. And how were the iron-lines produced in the absence of an iron? Long before I owned an iron, what I used to do (like other students) is to put all my shorts and shirts under my pillows. A day or two after sleeping upon the pillows, the iron-lines would be visible—making the clothes seem as if they have been ironed. This practice was popular for a long time. It became moribund when the charcoal iron was introduced. Using the charcoal iron is simple—by putting its base upon hot charcoals and after being heated up, the process of ironing commences. Nowadays, with the electrification of most of the town-lets and villages, many of the charcoal irons have been replaced by the electric irons.

In 1959, our class and the class before us went on an excursion to Aiyetoro Community. We visited the king's palace and the hydroelectric power station. Founded in 1954, Aiyetoro Community is the first religious community of its kind in

Nigeria. Its leader is revered like a king. The citizens there follow the rules and regulations to the letter. They eat the same kind of food. They wear the same quality of clothes. They buy and sell as regulated. They work and play as regulated. They marry as regulated. They build their own primary and secondary schools. Their main produce is fish which they export to Lagos in their motor boats, owned by the community. Their men and women are as diligent as the men and women in Ipepe.

Three days, we spent in Aiyetoro Community and after we had paid a courtesy call to the king's palace, we left the community and came home with an air of nobility.

Chapter Ten

A Hair's Breadth Escape

Nineteen hundred and fifty-nine is an amaranth. It is a year I must continue to remember as I remember other important incidents and accidents which I witnessed as I was growing up to occupy an infinitesimal spot on the surface of God's earth.

One unsuspecting famished day, my father decided to mend the roof of my mother's house that leaked whenever water from heaven was looking for a place to touch and wet. The roof had been left un-mended for some time and my mother would complain whenever my father came to her house to relish with gusto some of her finest and mouth-watering dishes. My father, a roofer, had learnt the art of roofing almost at the same time he became a piscatorial man.

My father had properly examined the damaged area of the roof and he had asked me to assist him and I had acquiesced to do so with little or no sign of moue. About ten minutes after the job had started, my father descended in order to obtain a string with which to tie the rafts. No sooner he left than I saw a python, emerging with an attempt to swallow me whole. Quietly, and with a subdued paroxysm of trembling that descended on me like a sledgehammer, hammering my heart with a put-putting sound, I descended from the roof and let my father know that I had had a hair's breadth escape from a killer that kills its prey by swallowing. I looked unfazed but inside of me, my heart was pounding as if the legless reptile had turned me into a chicken-hearted latchkey lad.

"A python is hiding among the rafts?" asked my father in a tone suggestive of some kind of disbelief, coated with ire.

"Yes, a python, a big one."

"Did it look pusillanimous?"

"Not a bit, father."

"Was it trying to attack you?"

"Exactly so. It was trying to pounce on me," I rejoined with an innocent wry.

"Are you sure this is a python."

"Yes, I am sure." My father had asked this question for two reasons. The first reason is that a python never pounces at its preys. It lunges at its prey and after adjusting it properly in its jaws, will begin to swallow it whole. But a carnivore like a tiger attacks by pouncing. The second reason is that my father knows full well that I had never seen a python before. I had heard and read about pythons, especially from D.O. Fagunwa's books. But never had I seen one before—not in a distance let alone as an uninvited nonentity in our house—my mother's house.

Taking his double-edged cutlass in his left hand and his spear in his right hand, my father gestured to me to show him where the thief of the broad daylight was hiding. The way he held to his weapons was like an ambidextrous warlord who was ready to battle to the last drop of his blood. As my best man was trying to find his way to the roof, the python saw an armed man and then started to glide away. My father quickly called upon one of his brothers for help as the snake jumped inside water and proceeded to swim away. My uncle who was versed in the world of serpents, raced after it, negotiating every turn and twist the legless animal tricked him into. After a race that nearly lasted one hour, my uncle got close to it enough and consequently pulled his trigger and hit it fatally on the head. That was the end of a venomous legless creature that came to kill a member of our family in a broad daylight. The reptile was given to my father's resident-visitor, Baba Seri, from Ijebu province who disclosed to the family how delicious the snake meat was. I was almost tempted to have a taste of it after it had been made for lunch.

While putting a finishing touch to the roof—now beautifully mended, my father said I am twice a lucky lad for having a hair's breadth escape within three years! My mother shivered with happiness that the reptile did no harm to me before its end came. How joyous my mama was—that I am not a victim of a legless thief is beyond my ken till today.

In 1960, the year Nigeria attained her independence, causing Britain to lower once and for all the Union Jack, replacing it with green-white-green flag, I graduated from Zion-Ipepe Primary School. Before graduation, I couched the following poem whose title is *Midnight Libation—Kolanut*:

Oh Olodumare (2ce)
This is your symbol of friendship
Camaraderie and hospitality
To your people, my kith and kin offered
That they may enjoy a life
Full of peace and friendship
Ase! Ase! (Amen! Amen!)

Soon after the poem was read to my contemporaries, the news wafted all over the littoral town-lets and villages that Chief Obafemi Awolowo was encouraging us to go to the Modern School (Junior High School) in order to become more qualified—as teachers. I was about to shed some tears of disappointment but sooner than expected the community elders advised me to go higher, saying, "The higher you go, the cooler you become educationally." So the idea and dream of becoming a local teacher after graduating from the Primary School was squashed and thrown into an impalpable gutter filled with mosquito larvae.

Despite what the menace the jiggers, the mosquitoes and the leeches posed, my primary school life is a paradise to remember.

In 1961, I went higher—educationally—to the Junior High School (Modern School) which the Zion and Ipepe communities and the Local Council at Okitipupa had approved to take place at Zion-Ipepe. Like the Primary School, I belong also to the pioneers, some of whom came as far away as Ijebu and Ondo provinces.

That year our history teacher told us about the deaths of Dag Hammarksjold of Sweden, the second Secretary General of the United Nations and Patrick Lumumba, the newly elected Prime Minister of Congo. Both of them were gentlemen of peace for their countries and for the world. Before his execution in 1961, Patrick Lumumba has the following to verbalize, "No brutality, mistreatment, or torture has ever forced me to ask for grace, for I prefer to die with my head high, my faith steadfast, and my confidence profound in the destiny of my country, rather than to live in submission and scorn of sacred principles…Do not weep for me my dear companion. I know that my country which suffers so much, will know how to defend its independence and its liberty. Long live the Congo! Long live Africa!"

Tears rolled down my cheeks as our history teacher was reading out Lumumba's quotations. The whole class thought Africa must have lost one her brave and downright politicians.

Toward the second half of 1962, I lost my immediate elder brother, Omolebi. At a very young age, he was already recognized by Ogun, Oshun, Oya and Olokun as a piscatorial star who could throw his net, left and right and catch fish—in abundance—when lest expected. He was one the financial edifices behind my education. He died in his sleep in Cameroon, and the cause unknown. I was heart-broken. The whole family was heart-broken. I could not fathom how a young man should plunge from my world of immortality to a satanic world of mortality. His departure, his disappearance from my *hello greetings and touch*, pained me to my spinal chord, shook me like a willow in the storm.

During the second quarter of 1962, the pioneering class of the Modern School went on an excursion to Ibadan, the prosperous capital of western Nigeria and the largest indigenous city in Africa. Our excursion took us to three places, namely the Tobacco Factory, the Brewery Factory and the Liberty Stadium. Ibadan is so big in area—so spacious that many of us wondered why it was not made the capital of Nigeria, putting aside Lagos which has no place to expand except the lagoon.

In Lagos, we visited the Coker Cola House at Ijora Causeway. We heard the news and saw the pictures of Apalara and his nine murderers. Apalara, a noted Muslim cleric was killed in Ebute Metta, Lagos in 1952 by nine *oro* cultists who hated his preaching against their cult. How many times they had warned him to stop meddling into their business, no one could tell for sure. But one day as he was railing against the practice of cultism in Nigeria, he was confronted by the cultists who struck him with their cutlasses. Consequently, his body was tied to a stone and then dumped it into the lagoon. The nine members of the cult were apprehended after some investigation, and sentenced to death by a Lagos court. They were hanged in 1953. Obviously, and without putting a square peg into a round hole, 1963 serves as the tenth anniversary of such first mass hanging in Nigeria. As the news circulated and the pictures shown, many believers inferred that 1953 would go down in history as the year when religious tolerance started in Nigeria.

As 1962 brought bad news to the family, so also it brought good news. Before the end of that year, my elder sister Christina Mebebije gave birth to twins—both boys. That lucky day, a day in the history of immortality, my sister and I had gone to fetch beetle larvae and had found a lot of them. She had hewed and axed more than three logs of wood during the process of searching for the larvae, delicacies, like roe (from chichlid/tilapia) that often made me bite my tongue to bleed while munching them. No sooner we got home than she delivered after a brief travail. The first to be born has the natural name, Taiwo, while the second who is always considered the

55

senior, according to the Yoruba culture and cosmological views, has the natural name, Kehinde.

At the beginning of 1963, there were many tests in various subjects. In other words, our teachers were now preparing us to become teachers who would go out into the world to impart knowledge and wisdom into others. An essay I vividly remember yielded me an excellent mark. The essay was about a hardworking family of three—husband and wife and their only daughter. They worked so hard that they had no time to perform the ritual dance, very crucial for one and all in the community. The starling knew they were in trouble, knowing full well they were in a community where everyone had to perform a ritual dance after a day's work. So as the head (the husband) of the family was resting upon his hammock one evening as the gorgeous sun was setting, the starling perched on a line. After a few minutes of preening, it started to sing. Sooner than expected, the head of the family started to dance. Not quite ten minutes later, he was joined by his wife and their only daughter. Thus they were able to do as a result hard-work what they had left undone. Reading the essay to the class, Jedo, our avid English teacher revealed that as the best essay I stand a chance to become a wordsmith. Alas, his prophecy has yet to come to pass. However, I always remember what he used to say, "Reading is good. Writing is creative."

In 1963 as the tintinnabulation of our success was being heard, we were told by our teachers and members of the communities that we were on the right path of becoming good teachers with our Junior High School Diplomas. In addition to this, and with some emphasis on a verbal noun and but, they asserted that going to Senior High School (Secondary School) would make us more qualified a teacher, and with a better pay.

THE EFFECT OF THE FALLOUT: Between 1960 and 1966, many people in Nigeria were suddenly taken ill. It was the traditionalists who first noticed the epidemic. By the time the scientists came out with their findings, the epidemic had been

56

prevalent in all the West African countries. What is this epidemic? What is the cause?

The questions went from lips to lips in urban areas. Those in the country had no idea of what was befalling them. They were simply suffering in silence. Seemingly, the scientists, most of whom were products of colonization, did not want to tell the source of the epidemic. But after much pressure from the citizens who were just waking up and removing from their visages gossamery veils of colonization, it became known that the cause of the epidemic, largely a whooping cough and some irritation in the eyes, coupled with dizziness, was the atomic underground test (fallout of the radioactive debris as a result of a nuclear explosion) carried out in Reggane, Algeria, in Sahara Desert by the French government.

I felt sick for weeks—coughing, retching and vomiting. The same ill-health put two of my siblings out of joint for six months.

The Organization of African Union (OAU) tried many times to make the French government pay a paltry sum of money to the afflicted. It was rumored that the French government had some money as compensation but the OAU has no account in its files of accountability. Should the African Union (AU) reopen the files? Is this part of what Wole Soyinka refers to as "The Open Sore of a Continent?"

Whatever might be the level of the OAU's weakness, the French government did not stop testing its nuclear bomb on Algerian soil even after the Algerian independence in 1962. However, with the help of the United Nations, the French government was able to respect the hue and cry of the OAU and the testing finally came to an end in 1966. Since then, coughing, retching and vomiting seem to have disappeared from the life of every member of my family.

Chapter Eleven

Ijebu-Ode Grammar School

Thus I decided to go once again higher—educationally and landed at Ijebu-Ode Grammar School, founded in 1913. The decision to attend Ijebu-Ode Grammar School is not solely mine. Let's put it this way: I was smitten by my father's ambition to study in his father's original province.

As 1964 saw me at Ijebu-Ode Grammar School, my spirit started thanking my teachers at the Modern School and the community elders for encouraging me to go higher—educationally. Ijebu-Ode Grammar School, one of the best post primary schools in the continent is a place of sound education—physically and spiritually. A few weeks after my registration, I wrote the following poem as a token of gratitude to my Junior High School teachers and the community elders:

Afternoon Libation—Orogbo (Bitternut)
O Olodumare (2ce)
This orogbo is your emblem of longevity
And semi-immortality
To your people, my kith and kin offered
That they may enjoy a life
Full of longevity and semi-immortality
Peace and Love
Ase! Ase! (Amen! Amen!)

I was staying with Uncle Reuben Ade-gboye, a professional town secretary who had come back from United Kingdom not quite six months before my arrival. He was a gentleman who was loved by many members of my parents' extended family life. But my staying with him was brief—sadly—as he (and his wife especially) thought prostration failed in my way of greetings.

Weeks after reporting me to my father, he found an alternative place for me. So I left—sadly but exceedingly was relieved that I was not forced by a spouse of an uncle who was demanding from me what my parents did not coerce me to do. My contemporary at Modern School, Fola who was also the prefect of the school teamed up with me and we both rented a flat at number 25 Alausa Street, not far away from the campus of Ijebu-Ode Grammar School. The house, with a big zenana, is owned by Alhaji Alausa, a prominent Muslim in Ijebu-Ode.

I discovered sooner than later that my science subjects such as chemistry and physics could not stand me in good stead. I was not well up in them. In order not to be at the bottom of the class, I started burning the candles at both ends. The upshot was positive.

Even in a prestigious Grammar School like Ijebu-Ode Grammar School, corporal punishment was still a weapon, used to teach the stubborn students lessons of good behavioral attitudes. The principal, Reverend E. Ade Osisanya (1958-1972), our highly qualified moralist, and a disciplinarian, believes in every form of punishment (as long as it helps the students act responsibly) as he believes in his gorgeous wife who also teaches in the same school. Odu, our senior tutor was the expert in charge of corporal punishment for mature students to which category I belonged. His style of flogging his victim was unique, witty and often than not dramatic.

One day, I left the classroom without notifying my class prefect. My class prefect reported me to my house prefect and my house prefect took the case to the senior tutor. I knew I had broken the rule. I knew there was a price to pay for this. I knew I had to prepare to pay the price.

The senior tutor invited me to his office. Before I got there, he had prepared two questions for me. The first one: "How come that you do not know as a mature student that it is compulsory to tell your prefect before you leave the class?"

"I did not see my class prefect by the time of leaving."

"You could have left a note for him," he said in the most eminently practical way.

I scratched my head, not knowing what lie to tell.

Then he asked his second question: "Which part of your body will you allow to enjoy my sweet honey?"

"My palm." And I stretched out my left palm and suffered in silence like a *Man.*

One by one I received his sweet honey—six of them. Each time he landed his cudgel on my palm, he would go to a nearby chink in his office to release the smoke from his pipe. Only he alone flogged with such a drama, conflated with a tight tic of a smile, and jokes.

The first time I came closest to Oyinbo (a white person) was at Ijebu-Ode Grammar School. I had seen one or two in Lagos and during my trip to Cameroon. And I remember seeing one before the demise of colonization. He was a D.O—District Officer, representing a District. He was on a mission to one of the villages under his administration. While trying to wade a brook, one of my relatives offered to carry him on his back—across the brook—as part of the hospitality, always extended to foreign visitors. But because he was burlier than my relative, my relative carried him with difficulty and was about to drop him inside the brook infested with leeches. Help came sooner than later and he was pronounced to be a lucky District Officer.

The Oyinbo man at Ijebu-Ode Grammar School was my English teacher, from Scotland. He was a good teacher. And I could not figure out why such a good teacher should be called a white man. He was a colorless man as my classmates used to tease him. The only thing white about him was his white shirt which he wore regularly because of the general belief that dressing in white is ideal in tropical weathers.

One conspicuous thing I remember about him is his beautifully carved nose. His nose is very similar to mine in pointedness. But his own, carved beautifully like an arch, could also be described as the vault of heaven, while mine could be described as a vaulted roof. This is what we have in common even if his name has escaped my memory. He loved Nigerian literature, still struggling for recognition at that time, and wondered how my passion for writing and chiaroscuro was growing from week to week.

Heavy Petting: Something happened that changed my opinion of the women's world. Or shall I say something that changed my opinion of the opposite sex and added the first lesson to my amorous treatment of my first girlfriend. Was it towards the end of 1965? I could not say precisely. One day, a few hours before the gloaming set in, and before the zodiacal light became a charming phenomenon, I was mooning away some hours that made me feel as if I was on the crest of the gorgeous sun that was sinking gradually behind the mahogany trees. It was during the rainy season and the nature seemed to be at its best. I was simply strolling and enjoying myself in a peaceful and quaint town whose people are always magnanimous and whose streets, roads and boulevards are invariably clean. Only once I saw, to my chagrin, an island of a huge cattle dung in the middle of the Ijebu-Ode--Lagos Road, the main thoroughfare in the town. Because no one saw any cow in sight, or at least a herdsman, how the knoll-like dung came about to form a smoky island in the middle of the road, remains a mystery till today. It was during the evening rush hour. Which means it caused both the in-bound and out-bound traffic to be diverted to a feeder road for the in-bound traffic and a service road for the out-bound traffic.

Leaving this beautiful sight behind me, curiosity quickly whisked me into captivity, stopping me from enjoying the invigorating weather. On setting me free, I veered to the vicinity

62

where my female English teacher (an American Peace Corps) was living. As I got closer to her compound I saw her husband's lips glued to her lips, and their necks rocking. Jesus save me, I thought they were in a scuffle in which neither wanted to cry for help. The need to go and call a police officer before I could be accused of witnessing the bruising of lips was bothering me ere my alter ego nudged me and said that the husband and the wife were erotically enjoying themselves in the name of petting and kissing. So they kissed and necked: necked and kissed. They necked and kissed each other until their hair became disheveled. After they finished the rubbing together of their lips, they succumbed to some dizziness but they were happy and apparently must have seen the seventh heaven. The wife, as well as the husband seemed satisfied, and were perspiring profusely. They were being intoxicated by heavy petting which was so foreign to me—the way they nearly swooned and yet felt at the top of the world! I was bemusedly lost. I need a rescuer.

My stomach was hooked by an admixture of bewilderment and elation as I jogged, walked, ran, and sometimes ran, walked and jogged till I reached Biodun's house, my senior at school— breathing heavily like a wood-hewer. Sitting down with my weight and sweat, I was looking like a youth who had seen a Holy Ghost on his/her way to the house of worship, and whose lips were yoked with a bar of chocolates, *and as soon as the chocolates melted into my mouth, down to my stomach,* I related to Senior Biodun what my eyes had witnessed.

Biodun, a literature student who always buries his head in European literature, a book-worm who knows less than what he should know in African literature, explained to me that what I had seen is heavy petting, an erotic body language, a kind of warm-up exercise to love making. And that all the nations around the world practice heavy petting. Why is it that my parents never indulge in it? Is it a warm-up exercise among the educated citified people? These are the two questions on my lips as I was leaving my senior's residence. However, I thought I have learned something novel even if I could not use it as yet. I could not use it as yet because I was out of my element when it comes to discussing heavy petting.

When I gave a second thought to what I had done, I started to nurse some kind of guilty conscience. Suppose the couple had seen me, I wouldn't have been able to look them straight in the eyes thereafter in the school. But they won't even need me to look them in the eyes. The bottom line is that I have prized open the gourd containing the sweet ingredients of their privacy. There is enough suppurating evidence to press a charge of violation against me. At best, they could make me redundant. For making me repeat the same class over and over again could be their own sweet pay-back. My compunction would continue to prick me on two fronts. One, for violating a family privacy, and acting like a voyeur. Two, for not heeding the warning of my parents: haven't they said that I should stay out of trouble? Don't buy trouble, for the price of paying a trouble could be embarrassingly high whenever it becomes a legal trouble. My conscience asked me to apologize for what I had done, for what I had done is wrong. And I did apologize, praying Creator-Philosopher Olodumare to always be my guide and guardian. Then I felt a sense of proud relief steal over me, understanding that this is the first blemish of my life, perching upon a fait accompli.

Another eyeful thing I saw my American female English teacher do is the crossing of her legs in the classroom. And whenever she did that the class would raise their eyebrows and murmur that crossing of legs by females is a white man's culture and not a Nigerian thing. I never crossed my legs before the Elders and I never saw my mother cross her legs. Crossing of legs by a married woman and allow a married man to step over them is a bag-eyed abomination, as far as I can remember. And whenever that happens, the man in question would be asked to pay a ritual fine. A heavy one, always.

Reverend Osisanya, a trained biblical gentleman of Heaven and Earth, ordained during the colonial time, is a circumspect principal who never spares the rod whenever anyone of the students crosses the line of propriety and stumbles inside the pitch of embarrassment. During his days in London and on becoming a parson, he had chosen the parsnip as his favorite vegetable. He is a rhetorician who is often considered a connoisseur among his closest parson-friends. Sticking out of his office window is a banner indicative of a clergyman standing always on ceremony. I fear him with awe. Everybody does. Had he heard a hint of my voyeuristic activity, I could have been the ugly-headed object of his sermon the following day. I would expect him to say, "Low and behold! A student was found yesterday wasting time watching a shadow in its nakedness while he should be busy reading his books. I cannot understand why a student from a god-fearing family in a humble environment should go to the extent of peeping at the private life of a family. He has forsaken the ethical values of this institution. Forsaken or not forsaken, he knows what he has done is preposterous. No one: I say no one can comprehend the lousy chutzpah that must have led him astray. At the close of this assembly, he will see the senior tutor immediately. The senior tutor will let him know what he has to do to bring honor and credit to his parents, his community and the nation."

If he did not ask me to stand up so that all the eyes in the hall could stare me out, it is because I am a first-time offender who is being given the benefit of doubt and hoping that I would be able to ward off any elfin nuisance (in the impertinent nonentity of the Satan) in the future.

Whenever a student commits what is being considered as a bad, bad behavior, the senior tutor would crack jokes, laugh, lament, and then allow his heart to bleed. But cracking jokes in the midst of corporal punishment is his moonlighting or extracurricular business. At worst, he would refer to his victims as recidivists with blockheads. At best, and with some glittering of teeth, he would refer to each one of them as tomorrow's leader on whose head lies the sole crown which so many people would like to wear, adding that the metonymy is the language of the crown, as the language of divinity is the language of the kingdom. Me and other classmates and indeed the entire student population often refer phraseologically to him whenever we see him, thusly, "Uneasy lies the head that wears the crown."

A VEHICLE NEARLY HIT ME. This incident occurred one late evening when Fola and I decided to pad around after some hours of swotting. We had gone as far as Itoro square of the town. On our way home, Fola decided to play having finished smoking his last stick of cigarette. He chose to jump on the rear of a slow-moving truck and then jumped off it as effortlessly as he could like a stunt man. It was a great fun to him. Regaling on his success as well as his youthful exuberance, he smiled winsomely like a gold medalist and then asked me if I could do as he had done. Without thinking with my own faculty, I riposted that I could do exactly as he had done. Thus I jumped onto the low-moving truck and jumped off it again. Again, he ran after the truck and again, he flew onto it and then flew down. A great fun, it seemed indeed. All this time, the driver of the truck seemed not to know what was happening at the rear of his truck. Convincing myself that I could do it again, I ran after the truck, jumped onto it and jumped off it, landing on my fours, injuring the ball of my left palm. As an on-coming vehicle was about to run over me, I rolled to the curb just in time. My heart was pounding that my skull was not smashed into pieces. A pall of regret hung over me and then descended upon me like a downpour. Fola came to me, thanking Creator-Philosopher Olodumare for saving my life. Ever since that day, I have promised myself never to follow anyone in a dangerous play even if I know I could excel in it. I should learn how to use my own faculty and not the faculty of others.

Reading the Holy Bible has never been my cup of tea. To that ilk, I do not belong. But it did become my cup of tea at Ijebu-Ode Grammar School. The reason was not clear. But I guess it is because of our religion tutor who said that he has read the holy book from Genesis to Revelation. Added to this information and looking up and down, I guess the cardinal reason why I started to read the Bible is the disclosure that the Bible was translated from English to Yoruba by a freed slave.

"A freed slave?" The entire class exclaimed, showing facial expressions such as a wry, a pout, a moue, a knitted brow and drooping lips.

"Yes, a freed slave and his name is Bishop Ajayi Crowther. He was the first African (freed slave) to be ordained the Anglican Bishop in 1864. Born in Osogun, Reverend Dr. Samuel Ajayi Crowther belonged to the Yoruba ethnic group. After his capture at the age of fifteen, he was released and started to work in Sierra Leone."

Our religion tutor taught us many good things about the first African linguist to be ordained the Anglican Bishop and I am among those who feel he should be awarded a posthumous Nobel Prize in literature. Since then I continue to wonder how he managed to translate an English Bible into Yoruba. That wonder is like a puzzle whose clue has not been found.

It was rumored, according to our tutor that the first Nigerian linguist and intellectual wanted to convert his people—meaning the Yoruba people to Christianity so that they could become partials without necessarily carrying the British passports. The reason for the rumor is that the Church of England saw in him a high degree of pragmatism, sensibility and an unbelievable sense of organization, thinking that every Yoruba man and woman is like him. But a number of the kings rejected the idea of becoming aliens in their homeland—without demure.

As I was struggling to become one of the best in the class so also I was praying for the end of the civil war that commenced in 1967. It started after my third and last trip to Cameroon, the first being 1964 and the second was 1966.

Nineteen sixty-four: that was the year I first traveled from Nigeria for Cameroon. My sisters (Christiana and Maria) and other members of my family were enthusiastically happy to see me. I was also happy to see them. They treated me like a situational prince, although every son and daughter with Yoruba blood can claim to be a prince and a princess, respectfully. The year, 1964 was the first time I felt the great impact of a collective love of my family members. I was blessed to have surprised them. I was blessed to have made the journey even if they did not pat me on the back for making such a journey alone at a young age. Every word and greeting that proceeded from their mouths was indicative of love and the power to love. I think the reason they are so happy to see me is because of my excellent school report. They know that I have invariably sought to be one of the best in the school—from the time we were together till the time they lost me to the *Republic of Words and Letters*.

My feeling as a result of that experience is that when siblings live together, eat together, grow together, rejoice together, cry together, fight together, they do that in the name one pedigree and a strong bond of love. Any reason or attempt to sever that bond of love will be painful. And for my sisters, to leave Nigeria with their husbands for Cameroon is like breaking a family covenant and throwing it in a pond that generates a suppurating pain. Thus seeing me in their midst when least expected, replaced the pain with abundant joy: the joy, likened to a bolt from the blue.

Added to the above is the fact that my first journey to Cameroon afforded me the opportunity to see other towns and cities such as Buea Edea, Douala, Tiko and Yaoundé. From Tiko, a port town at the slopes of Mount Cameroon, a family friend and I went on a tour to the port town of Victoria (now Limbe since 1982) and its romantically beautiful botanical garden, said to be the flagship in West Africa.

Two weeks prior to the second quarter-holidays in 1966, the school invited one of the best traveling theaters in the world. The name of the theater is Kola Ogunmola Travelling Theater, under the directorship of Kola Ogunmola. I had been hearing of Ogunmola but I have never attended anyone of his performances. Why I had been dying to see him in action is that rumors had it that whenever he spoke, his voice would echo and reecho for minutes. True or false? I was so blessed when our principal announced that he would be coming to add some spicy grains of paradise to our literature class.

It was the school's Assembly Hall, full to capacity even before the show began by eight o'clock. The bell rang. There was an eerie din that put everyone to a sleep-like silence. Then the female dancers trooped out from behind the stage. The multicolored costumes upon their shiny ebony bodies uncontrollably whetted my appetite to the theatrical point of infatuation. However, I managed to control myself like an actress for what I could not endure like an actor. That was the first time my manhood would borrow trouble ever since I broke my voice. The manner the girls danced was wrapped with twists and turns, conflated with charming and finesse and I was enveloped with euphoria or was it tantalization and transported to a terra incognita of make-belief world of dramatis personae. "Are these human dancers? Or are they angels in human bodies?" I nudged and asked the person sitting next to me. He had no clue, for he also was mesmerized by the way those dancers were twisting, waltzing and jazzing their bodies to the rhythms, melodies and harmonies of the drumming.

About fifteen minutes later, emerged the king of charms and vials. The colored lights poured over him. His basso profundo and yodeling voice sent the audience to the seventh heaven. Such was the situation. As I woke up from such a reverie and putting myself together, I started wondering why the school could not invite the traveling theater on a regular basis. Many of my contemporaries believe that having Kola Ogunmola, Chief Hubert Ogunde, Duro Ladipo, Prince Seven-Seven, Muraina Oyelami, Jimoh Buraimoh and their like to perform once a year in our literature and English classes is better than those foreign literature books that do not depict the temperaments, the sensibilities, the nature, the experiences and the political, economic, historical, religious, anthropological and sociological circumstances of the Nigeria people. We all long for an immediate birth and firm establishment of Nigerian literature.

Two other artists I have been dreaming of seeing in action are Duro Ladipo and Prince Seven-Seven. I have had much about the magic power beneath the tongue of Duro Ladipo— that whenever he opened his mouth to speak, a roar of thunder (Shango) would emerge, to be followed by fire that burns without fuel. He is the sole ventriloquist with more than five vocal sounds. Alas, I never see him in action before his death in 1978.

But I had the rare opportunity to watch Prince Twins Seven-Seven in 1969 at the German Goethe Institute in Lagos. It was a matinee event. He is the most versatile and the most talented of all the Nigerian artists, for he can draw much as he can paint, dance, choreographs, mime, sing, write and dramatize. From all accounts, he belongs to the most versatile artists the world has produced. Oh man, this genius of a man is great. He is exceptional. When on stage, his scherzo is like that of a classic palace minstrel, and when he narrates, one feels the presence of the legendary Queen Scheherazade.

Rumors had it that his passed-away twin brothers and sisters must have propelled him to the apex of his profession. Having heard much about Oshogbo Art School that produces all these men of artistic geniuses, I have invariably been thinking of visiting the school with the hope of learning the art and then turning some of my poems into visual arts that I can touch with sensibilities. Putting down something (in form of painting or drawing) from your head that no one but you alone can interpret is like a charm whose source is known only to the charmer. How I wished I had had the opportunity to visit this phenomenal school!

In 2005, Prince Twin Seven-Seven was named UNESCO Artist for Peace by UNESCO Director General, Koichiro Matsuura. The ceremony was attended by Chief Olusegun Obasanjo, the President of the Federal Republic of Nigeria.

I dreamt one day and saw every Nigerian woman and man acting. On asking the Lord of dreams the interpretation of my dream, he tersely told me that there is joy and life in acting, adding with a winsome smile that acting brings life and laughter to the heart that acts and to the heart that sees one acting.

In spite of the war that nearly shook my will and the wills of my contemporaries, I managed to put myself together, ready for the final examinations, conducted by the West African Examinations Council. The Nigerian office of the West African Examinations Council was at Yaba and Chief Popoola, a cousin of mine, worked there. The sweet success came the following year. I had passed all my papers save two. I have no explanation why those two papers jumped out of my catch. *Maybe I could have caught them like my father had I been a fisherman.* And I laughed rather confidently as though I would be given another chance to retake the exams. Would there be a tabula rasa for me? I wondered as though lost in thought.

At the end of every year, the principal of the school, Reverend Osisanya, used to give a series of lectures. This is a tradition ever since he joined the school as the upstanding head of the school and CMS chapel in 1961, or thereabout. One which he gave and which I have not forgotten is the following: "Your best case scenario as you are going into a larger world is this: you must learn how to choose the right words that would immortalize the world as the world stumbles in its attempt to find the right words for its moral survival." The way he looked, the way he spoke made me believe that he was a prophet who believed the world would decay without a moral compass.

THE KONGI HARVEST: One Friday afternoon which should be counted as one of the two Fridays before I said goodbye to Ijebu-Ode Grammar School, I visited my cousin Kehinde Popoola in Lagos. After a quick supper that lasted less than one hour in a bukaria, (bukaria, an indigenous restaurant) he told me that the Kongi Harvest by Wole Soyinka was going to be premiered that evening. He was excited but I was much

71

more curious and excited than him—to see a man whose name we heard many times but not met.

In January 1968, a month prior to the announcements of the school results, I wrote the following ditty to thank my parents, my brothers and sisters, uncles, aunts, cousins and other relatives:

Rain Unstoppable

Rain will fall
Waters above confluence with
Waters below
Rain will fall
Scared, a rain maker
Fleet-footed
Stumbles and falls
Ere he could lock
The overflowing wells above
Could anyone stop rain from falling?

THE LOSS OF A MESSIAH: In April 4, 1968, one of the local newspapers carried the news that one of our overseas big brothers, whose voice, basso profundo, used to fall like a sledgehammer on the ears of his hearers and listeners, had been assassinated by a demented racist. His picture was not available in the local newspaper, nor did I hear a lot of him from the local radio. Meeting two of my friends later that evening, it was revealed to me that the assassinated fighter of human rights and equality for one and all was Dr. Martin Luther King, Junior. I went back home knowing nothing of him other than the world had lost a Messiah and the fact he had left behind—for the world a prophetic dream, containing among other things a table of contents of character—as if he was born a Yoruba who values character more than anything given to man by Divinity-Philosopher Olorun.

Chapter Twelve

The Child is Shifting for Himself

After searching for jobs from companies to companies and from ministries to ministries, for almost ten months, I got a cushy one through the help of Uncle and Chief Popo-ola, at the Federal Ministry of Economic Development and Reconstruction. With happiness pulsating in my heart, I looked intently into the glistering sun and said that I had found myself free from eating the bread of dependence. The ministry occupied the 24th and 25th floors of the Independence Building, the tallest structure but one in Nigeria. (The Independence Building, silhouetted against the Race Course, serves as a major attraction for anyone who wants to gaze heavenwards at an object other than a heavenly body.) It quickly occurred to me that the idea of going higher—educationally still sticks to me like a limpet—job-wisely.

Standing on the 26th floor of the building where the machines including the air-conditioners are kept, one sees the nakedness of the proverbial Lagos Lagoon, stretching to Ipepe and other littoral town-lets and villages. I will remember it is on this lagoon I was delivered by Divinity-Philosopher Oshun some five decades ago. How many times have I bathed in it, I don't know. But I know many people have dipped their bodies inside it since time immemorial. I know it has quenched the thirst of young and old. I know it has washed away the blemishes of the unfaithful spouses. I know it has washed ashore the stolen goods from the capsized barges and ships of the thieves, smugglers and pirates. I know it has washed away the blood-stains from the weapons of murders. I know thousands of fishers have fished on it since its existence. Oh nostalgia, don't flirt with me. I just want to know what I think I know. I know you know what I know that Lagos Lagoon is a water-mark (nay landmark) of indestructibility.

Working as a clerical officer with a High School Diploma is not the best thing for me at that time but it was the best thing for the citizens of Ipepe who believed working in the tallest building in Lagos meant it is my destiny to always go higher—educationally and work-wisely. I had a good time working with my co-clerical officers. The interaction was good. Lagos presented such a superb milieu.

In 1969, I lost Fola, my contemporary at Zion-Ipepe Modern School and Ijebu-Ode Grammar School. His death was sad. It came when least expected. I searched the ingredients of immortality inside the calabash bowl of my soul and I realized that more than one ingredient is missing.

Chasing svelte girls in Lagos nearly became my business without a business plan. Sylphs and girls with extra-ordinary body-languages from over one hundred ethnic groups in the country are not hard to find in Lagos. I saw a lot of them. I talked to some of them but I was unlucky to have any of them as my permanent girlfriend until I was able to put my longing into continence.

In my company most of the time were Michael, alias Mete, and Eliam. Apart from the perfumed ministry girls, we came across many beauties in many of the Lagos Districts such as Ijora and Ajegunle and we nearly regarded ourselves as lady-killers. I was adrift to many subterranean and labyrinthine alleys and cul-de-sacs. Some even led me to the precincts of the *Departments of Demand and Supply*. Was it a kind of curiosity, the mother of knowledge?

In Ijora, one of my cousins was heard saying that the furniture I had in my room was not mine. He uttered the back-biting statement as he was trying to woo the same woman, already in love with me. My humble pride was wounded knowing full well that a cousin of mine could make such a pronouncement in a metropolis where there are hundreds and hundreds of pretty angels. As luck would have it such a stab on my back did not stop the woman in question to say yes to life in my favor. Today, even if I had brushed the pronouncement into a dustbowl, regarding it as a balderdash, the breeze fanning my tongue and my ears nearly knocked me down, and the fondant in my mouth nearly made me retch on hearing the bunkum for the first time—coming from my own cousin and made known to me by my own cousin.

In the blind alley of Lagos city life, in the middle of a thorough-fare, encircled by a traffic island, I found myself waylaid by nadir. As if Michael and I could not have enough of those chocolate girls, we allowed ourselves to be charmed by the Indian girls as appeared in the Drum magazine and other national and international journals. These journals were often inundated by Indian advertisers selling talismans designed to find girlfriends for boys and boyfriends for girls. Rumors of the talismans and their efficacies were rife all over the country. It was as if the Yoruba goddess of love had moved her headquarters to India. Peddlers of rings and amulets were many in Nigeria but they must be ten times less in number than their counterparts in India. How far the thought of using a talisman to obtain a girl's friendship had affected my psyche at that time, I can't say for sure. But I was led into believing the advertisers. After some period of time, I found out that those the advertisers and their spells were a kind of hoaxes. But they took hold of me for a while ere I was disillusioned. And enlightenment became my lot.

Chapter Thirteen

My Father, Oh My Father

In October 1970, Chief Reuben Ojagbuwa Ogunyemi of Ipepe, the miracle town, succumbed to death after a prolonged illness. Sadness and sorrow tore me apart like the picture of a ragged old beggar or a homeless youth dressed in tatterdemalion. Life began to torment me. I began to slough off my skin of inanities and simplicities regarding immortality. A son had missed the important words of advice of his dear father which his dear father had accumulated during his living years. I began to fight for the singularity and indivisibility of a life that is no more palpable. An important and irreplaceable ingredient of immortality from inside the calabash bowl of my soul is missing. Life is no longer the same, losing the foundation of the family. This becomes clear to me. I wept like a sheep without a shepherd. It is hard to comprehend life when ingredients after ingredients are chipping away. The cub's heart was broken as the lion joined the long pedigrees of his ancestors. It was now vivid to me that I was at the nadir of all the hopes I have been assembling at the back of my mind. "Oh life, what are you doing to me? You killed my grandmother, you murdered my grandfather, you killed my brother, you killed my friend, you killed my father. Oh life, what are you doing to me?" I cried unrestrainedly, stomping the floor and creating the sound like that of a pachyderm—running.

Each time I stepped out into the street, I would hear the voice of my thought asking me to disappear for a while: that I should leave Ipepe, leave Ode-Omi, leave Lagos and seek a refuge elsewhere. "Leave while Olodumare will make those workers of nightmare vanish before your coming back to the land whose sun scratches your back and whose moon always tickles your imagination and your liquid regards."

The question of what to do sometimes always deflated me whenever I thought of how to overcome the weaknesses of human nature. I think very often of utopia where every creature assumes the skin of purity, next to the aura of holiness, feeling the full weight of incessant dreams of love, peace, unity and philosophy of closing the gap between heaven and earth.

I consider this spiritual thought of warning as a godsend. At this point, my reflection had identified itself with visibility, while my reminiscence had identified itself with invisibility. Thus I am now a child wedged between visibility and invisibility. This is how I must live, continue to live in order to allow those workers of nightmares seek their self- destruction in the lake of bonfires. I am both visible and invisible—appearing and disappearing. Anything short of this is non-sequitur, adds to nothing and must be allowed to wither in confinement.

This is the way I look at it. If visibility should be my past, I want invisibility to be my present and immortality my future. In order to upgrade myself to this phenomenal plane of existence, I need love which is the ruler of all arts. I need songs too, because songs charm love, and both are seen to be juxtaposed in the heart of hearts.

How do I start? This is another question. I am aspiring to inculcate into my faculty Chief Awo's philosophy of *doing something or doing nothing and dying in shame*. At the same time, I am holding to my father's first philosophical aphorism that says *it is more honorable to do a few things that make people happy than to do a lot of things that make none happy*. Yet his second philosophical aphorism is as important as the former: *Any lore that widens people's horizons and presents food for thought is the beginning of philosophy*.

Whenever I went to the office and saw the faces which the moribund civil war had brought back to the fold of one Nigeria in diversity, my heart would leap for joy—desiring more grains of paradise to chew. My body would be drenched with the feeling of goodness that Nigeria would grow from strength to strength—shaking off the dust of greed, foolishness and immaturity after ten strong years of ominira (independence.)

The bottom line is that there is no way I can turn myself into a monster, a goddess, or a fish and live inside water like Oshun. Terra firma is the sole place I know even if I was born inside a fishing boat—with the help of Oshun. I must continue to bear this dual skin of visibility and invisibility—a panacea for my survival.

I envy a multicultural milieu where everything is colorful like the flowering plants in my father's yard. I envy a society which lives in peace—sharing—giving—and pacifying the belligerent—changing them as the missionaries have changed our house. I like a heterogeneous metropolis which is striving to make something phenomenally meaningful of its heterogeneity. I like a world that uses the **word** to find the quintessence of the creation and its spiritual wellness. I should be able to touch and heal in the name of Jesus Christ of Nazareth, with the permission of the everlasting God. If I should follow the aesthetic values of the Elders, I will not fall even if I stumble. A time has come when my community needs something from me. Oh God, you should help me give back to my community that which my community desires, and to the world that which the world badly needs—*unity and faith, peace and progress. Arise O Compatriots, Nigeria's Call, Obey.*

The first day I stepped my feet on the carpet of my office, from my look and the way I pouted, everyone who saw me could easily infer that I was ill at ease. I had carried a burden, a heavy one to work, and thank God, some of my co-workers helped me to share it. They believe in the saying that a problem shared, is a problem halved.

Chapter Fourteen

The Holy-gourd

It is good to know one's culture, for culture is the totality of one's being. What I had wanted to know from my father is the power behind the holy-gourd. Many times I would see my father standing up and facing the sun as the heavenly body was rising and covering the universe with its illumination. In the hand of my father would be a vial, a holy-gourd. Soon, he would open his mouth and start to pour out incantations such as these:

I thank you, Oh Olodumare for your blessings
I thank you for seeing this light of yours before me
Let your blessings continue to shine upon me and my family
As the sun shines upon every creature in your creation.

You've made me part of the water:
Therefore no one quarrels with the water without drinking it
You've made me part of the air:
Therefore no one quarrels with the air without inhaling it
You've made me part of the earth:
Therefore no one quarrels with the earth without treading it.

No bird in its flight has ever struck its head against a tree
Let no member of this family lose his/her head

Whenever the sun rises, its rays perch upon the trees.
Let me perch upon my enemies as a sign of victory upon them. (Ase)

After the incantations, my father would toss some of the contents in the vial to the ancestors. Sometimes, he would put in his mouth the liquid content and spray the atmosphere with it.

There are other incantations which are said to ward off evil-doers or workers of nightmares. Many of them cannot be revealed and if revealed there will be "life imprisonment under the tunnel."

What is then the holy-gourd? I always ask myself before Pa Bola, one of the family's diviners explained it to me. The holy-gourd is a symbol of necessity conferring material, spiritual and mystic benefits.

Chapter Fifteen

The Effects of Lagos on a Child-Boy

Lagos was a city of about one million inhabitants—comprising of the so-called black, white, brown and yellow human beings, by the time I came to know it *properly* in 1967. But I did not claim to know it *properly* until I had the opportunity to visit all its twenty-five districts in a circumambulatory manner, in 1968. The following are the principal districts: Agege, Ajegunle, Apapa, Ebute-Metta, Eti-Osa, Ijora, Ikeja, Ikotun, Ikoyi, Ilupeju, Isolo, Kosofe, Lagos Island, Maryland. Mushin, Obalende, Ojo, Oshodi, Shomolu, Surulere, Victoria Island, Yaba. Due to the oil boom that occurred immediately after the end of the hostilities of the civil war, Lagos experienced unprecedented population explosion, untamed economic growth and unstoppable influx of immigrants from the country.

Life is swinging here. The atmosphere is swimmingly peaceful here. I will not find my job beyond this pulsating metropolis. I am not going to Benin-City, Enugu, Ibadan, Kano, or the Garden-City of Port-Harcourt. Any city beside Lagos will be regarded as the back of beyond. This is what I said to myself while searching for jobs in 1968.

The nightlife is cool and wooing. Everywhere there was a kind of entertainment, including those tricksters who had no shame to say that they would turn your ten kobo into ten millions of nairas. Music could be felt around every corner of the street. And you can while away your time from dusk till dawn without anybody stopping and asking you for a sacrifice or tithe of one kobo.

The most prominent street performer in Lagos is Benjamin Aderounmu, the one-man band-singer with a banjo as his only instrument and a mouth organ. His musical name, mythical as heaven and popular as earth is Kokoro. No one hears his voice once would refuse to hear it twice. His voice is mellifluous. It is engaging, adorable, proverbial and uplifting. For how long he has been playing in Lagos I have no idea I could call my own. There are three versions of the musical story about him. The first version of the story is that he was a former palace minstrel, going from palace to palace before he decided to spend the rest of his life in Lagos. The second version of the story is that Olorun wants everyone to know that a handicapped person can make a living. The third version of the tale is that Olodumare woke him up from among the dead and makes him a singer extraordinaire. There is no way to prove or disprove any of the three versions of the story. The three versions of the story are true and they will remain true until one rises and conducts an interview with him.

Nineteen sixty-eight is the first time I saw him at Oyingbo, his wonted place of entertainment. But that was not the first time I would hear news about his amazement—his gift of gab. That day in 1968, I was on a bus going from the Island to the mainland of Yaba, one of the chief arrondissements in Lagos. He was surrounded by a concourse of people. While some stood still listening to his music with rapt attention, some were shaking their heads in apparent enjoyment of his banjo sound and the songs pouring from his mouth.

At the end of that day, I said to myself that I would have to see Kokoro, the fantastic roadside musician at close quarters and enjoy his enchanting songs, his proverbial ditties and roundelays. I told a few friends of mine how I saw the maestro inside a bus and my plan to see him at close quarters. Some of my friends said that God has been so wonderful to have blessed the maestro who is a blind man and still able to perform like an able-bodied musician.

For almost a week, I had no time to visit Kokoro and enjoy his ear-pleasing music, for I was occupied by my longing to find a job I could call my own. One hazy Monday, as the sun landed its therapeutic rays on the surrounding red and white mangroves,

I decided to visit my uncle Hosea Aiyelo (May his soul rest in perfect peace) at Oyingbo Leventis Store where he worked as a technician. It was about 2 pm when I reached Oyingbo, visiting the one-man band musician before visiting my uncle. The singer was already swarmed by a host of admirers. Some were shaking their legs, bums and legs. Some were swinging their necks like the Ethiopian traditional dancers. In no time at all, his proverbial ditties started to sink into my sun-baked head. In no time at all, I started to act like a reveler, for I was now charmed and drugged by his music. Wow, this creature of a man could sing. He could sing and dexterously play his banjo. He sings mellifluously like a nightingale and whistles amorously like a redstart.

Words, phrases, sentences, metaphors and ironies will not be adequate to express what I witnessed and enjoyed that day. My experience was simply beyond description and deception. And I must quickly confess that he made my day that Monday afternoon after listening to his music for one hour and a score. My physiognomy was aglow with happiness and exultation by the time I got to my uncle's office. He did not ask me why I was a different person (with a glowing mark on my countenance) that day nor did I disclose to him why I was at the top of the world despite the fact that I was till jobless, looking for a job I could call my own. He is the second one-man band I have ever met.

This stanza I will continue to remember about the maestro:

I wear my destiny like a cap
What I was yesterday is not what I am today
No one knows tomorrow except Olodumare
The Author of Life and Death
This is my destiny, fellow humans
I am wearing my destiny like a cap
For life is shrouded in mysteries and vicissitudes.

Kokoro, a music legend and unsung hero in the metropolis of Lagos lives forever. Music has become his democracy without a government. Music has opened his innermost vision. Music has enlightened him and put him ahead of mortality. Music has brought him closest to the celestial hymns. Music has become his open-air shrine of worshipping Creator-Philosopher Olodumare. Music has been his open-palm secret of survival.

Rumors wafting in the air—around the nooks and crannies in the country is that the Federal Government of Nigeria has abandoned an important and hard-working musician. The rumor-mongers, some of whom are flibbertigibbets, allege that Kokoro has tremendously contributed to the social atmosphere of the country and should not be abandoned like an over-used dashiki. The rumor-mongers including me suggested that a letter of encouragement be written to the Gowon's government asking him to come to the plight of the self-made musician, scraping a living.

As the rumors turned into talk-of-the-town and the talk-of-the-town turned into a proverb, everyone seemed to be saying that if Kokoro were to be an American citizen, he could have been surrounded by men and women of timber and caliber: people with lots of beans who would raise his musical status to the firmament and ultimately lead him to the Musical Hall of Fame.

But this was 1968. The only union, capable of writing such a letter is the Nigerian Union of Musicians, in which Kokoro is an invisible maestro, sitting on a three-legged chair, pent up by a feeling of loss of sight. If the Union of the Nigerian Musicians had written a letter, the Gowon's government could have argued that it could not help any artist who could not help himself/herself at a time when it was just inhaling and exhaling enjoyably a lease of fresh air, found at the end of the tunnel—having survived a national suicide of mass destruction in the sick name of civil war.

If money in life is what man can think of making himself happy, he is wrong without the female children of God. Thus Lagos social life is incomplete without women. I saw this. I felt this as I padded from one part of the metropolis to another. I

86

saw that there are four categories of women in Lagos. The first category is the super Lagos Girls who are neither girls nor madams. They are the players, the movers, the shakers and the high grammarians of the city's present tense—the like of those described in Jagua Nana by Cyprian Ekwensi. The second category, like the first one is psychedelic. They are the belfries of the Lagos Stock Exchange. They are the Lady-Girls, the like described by Victor Olaiya as Omopupa. The third category is similar to the second one. They are the coquettish ones, the ones described by Ebenezer Obey and King Sunny Ade in their repertoires. The fourth category is the Market Women. They are the feeders and mothers of the buyers. Their brains are very sharp. They know the addition, multiplication and subtraction formulas without going to school. They cannot be cheated by anyone even if he/she is a college mathematics major. Whosoever attempts to cheat them, will bring shame and ridicule upon him or her. This category also includes women who own the bukarias, the indigenous restaurants which have always fed the beaus of the city including ministry secretaries.

The following is the dialogue I overheard from two diners in a bukaria, not far from Race Course: one in civvies and the other, a uniformed soldier:

Civilian: They should turn this bukaria into a hotel and make the diners pay more.
Soldier: Why?
Civilian: Because the meals here are as delicious as those in good hotels.
Soldier: For my money, they should simply increase a bowl of amala and create more space for the customers.
Civilian: That makes sense. If I may ask you, why do you come here wearing your military uniform?
Soldier: Because the country is still at war.
Civilian: Must you wear a uniform in a peaceful place like this where there is little or no rumor of war?

Soldier: By wearing my uniform shows we should be vigilant. It shows that war is still going on.

Civilian: When will the on-going war be ended?

Soldier: Honestly, I don't know.

Civilian: You should know, knowing full well that the war is caused by the army who are supposed to be in their barracks.

Soldier: It is too early to tell. Meanwhile, let's enjoy to the full our diners.

Civilian: Good to confab with you. I hope we meet another time.

Soldier: I hope so. I hope the war must have stopped by then.

The way the civilian dressed and the way she conversed with the soldier and the way her hips obeyed the drumming rhythms of her footsteps as she galloped—with the stiletto shoes with silver studs, was more than a hint to me that she is a Lagos woman.

Lagos ladies are *nulli secondus*. They break nothing. They tie nothing. They loose nothing. They hold no prisoners. They are as free as the lagoon breeze. They are the shakers and movers of any life that walks upon the earth. They are *jayejaye*—life-revelers. They swing between verbal nouns and participial adjectives. Most of them grew up as gilded youths who are living in a gilded cage. That they had some ladyfied secrets, cannot be disputed. But these secrets as classified as they are, no man dare blow the gaff about them. I must add that not every one of them is a feme sole. As a matter of fact, majority of them are either engaged with the rings of immortality or married. The married ones (the feme coverts), even with the responsibilities of a matrimony in their hands, are very active, and always showing the feme soles that they cannot be pushed to the back-burners.

The indelible effect on me when I got to know one (*touch-me-not*) of them was romantic as it was poetic as the nocturne from the lips of a drowning but rescued sailor. More revelation about this special one (this *touch-me-not*) I know will be made circumstantial later.

Their weaknesses are based on the fact that they are susceptible to sugar-coated lips of men who can boast of millions of dollars in their piggy banks.

What makes the Lagos women special is hard to describe. This is because they are not only the beau ideal, they are also legendary and versatile in all things pertaining to social life and high society under the vault of heaven. But the most noticeable thing is the *gele* (the headgear.) The headgears are designed in various sizes and colors. There are many styles and names. They are flamboyant. Only these women in Lagos adorn their heads in this fashion, compared to other women in all the continents of the world. Some are called Mama Ibeji, Mama Eko, Saturday Night, Monday Eye-catcher, Touch-me-not, Rainbow, Crescent, Full Moon, Sky-is-the-limit, Love-It, Do-me-good, The Best, Wake- me-up, Sunshine, Lagoon Breeze, Atlantic Crest, Bar-Beach, No Blemish, All-Seasons, Vault of Heaven, Grains of Paradise, Essence of Bergamot, et-cetera.

Looking at these headgears from all angles, one will find out that the most popular and perhaps the most remarkable and adorable, which is not necessarily the most expensive one, is the sky-scraper (*onilegogoro*). This name reflects the independence celebrations of 1960 and the independence building, the tallest sky-scraper in Lagos with its twenty-five floors.

For what it is worth, *touch-me-not* is the only one I had attempted to touch. But the plan fell through on knowing that somebody was already touching her. Oh pretty Priscilla whose soft and sweet voice can be likened to the voice of a cherub or a nymphet, is a young woman of noble manners. She was the first woman at that time who possessed the courage to invite me to her birthday party despite the fact that her boyfriend was in attendance. Her lips could be likened to the magnetic hook under the chest of a tropical jellyfish. Her breath was like the mint coming from the scientific combination of eucalyptus and the essence of bergamot, fortified by the flavors from the grains of paradise. Whenever she spoke, her speech would sink into my imaginary head like a bullet of spell. And whenever she stopped speaking, she was like a dumb whose smile woke up a lover from a comatose. This reminds me of a tale of three sisters locked in an eternal triangle love. One of the sisters succeeded in killing the lover with her infectious smile and then used the same infectious smile to wake up the lover. Consequently, she married the lover-man. But because the number of the sisters involved in this eternal triangle is three as opposed to two, I always refer to this type of emotional relationship as *Triple H.*

I was in a comatose and there was no one to wake me up with her infectious smile. So the reality is here before my nose. The lucky beau was there before me—already. Playing second fiddle seemed to be the sole choice left for me. But I saw her everyday as we worked in the same Federal Ministry of Economic Development and Reconstruction. This is why I am lucky but not so lucky like the lucky beau who owns the honey-love of her heart of hearts.

One blessed Tuesday, in the hush of the morning after the long weekend sanctioned by Easter holidays, I met Priscilla in her office chatting with a friend of hers who was also an omnivorous reader. All of a sudden her friend said, "We are good civil servants, pretty, able and willing to serve our government, we ask you to grant us our wishes to continue to chat."

Nostalgically, my head swung towards my parent's house, searching for a similar but wittier aphorism that could keep both passionate friends chatting and laughing and whining like a legendary flirt whose secret of loving spell-bound his captives to an amazing smile of helplessness and surrender. The power of reasoning aphorisms in my parents' house cannot be under-estimated.

Then came an intruder. It was a short-lived blanket of silence and the two pretty friends were sitting upon the silence, sharing the silence of reason, while at the same time luxuriating in the sound of silence as produced by reason.

90

Ere I could find a suitable metaphor or an irony to entertain them in the name of raillery or pleasantry, or something out of nowhere that could sound like a Yoruba aphorism or ethics, Priscilla's boss, the Permanent Secretary, emerged from his cozy office, and having greeted him nervously, I vanished into the thin air that brought me back to my wonted place in the Records section of the Ministry's Registry.

This omnivorous Fulani girl-woman from Middle Belt of Nigeria, speaks like an intellectual and reasons like a feminist. In the eyes of the beholder, she is blessed with eight signs of beauty—gorgeous hair, a good set of white teeth, narrow ankles, small caressing fingers, slopping shoulders, broad pelvis, thin and smooth forearms and a slender neck garlanded with folds of skins. Her world has no room for diffidence and hebetude and one unkind day, I troubled myself so much that I felt infatuation was teasing me to give her a bunch of hebes. Through thick and thin, I put my infatuation to ridicule and a bag-eyed shame. The only thing I thought I could have given her could have been a heavy petting and that too, I have avoided by flying into a passion in lieu of felicity, debonairness or Pollyannaism. Thus I survived two temptations, one after another.

An avid reader she is indeed. In her hands, I saw a new book each week. Her avidity is second to none among the Lagos women who often force their hips to dance with the put-putting sounds of their footsteps. I learned much from her intellectual ingredients. Even if she does not wholly belong to the high grammarians of the city's present tense who are versed in the game of serendipity and indispensability, she is number one who had given me, as well as wishing me, the joy of reading for pleasure. From her I often remember what Jedo, one of my tutors at Junior High School often says, "Reading is good. Writing is creative."

When, where and how the Lagos women acquired this unique headgear is a secret which yet is to be demystified. However, the index fingers (mostly of historians and other researchers) are pointing to Queen Moremi of the holy city of

Ile-Ife. Was she the first woman who first adorned her head with this type of headgear? I don't know. I can't tell. I don't want to conjecture anything that may be far and false from the realm of actuality and verisimilitude. But time will tell. Wait and let the time become the teller.

Chapter Sixteen

Study Leave Without Pay

In 1971, the news of the Golden Fleece was brought to the doorstep of my studies. I was curious much as I was excited. In no time at all, I obtained my passport—with insignificant payola and started preparing to fly over the might of the Sahara Desert, fly over the Mediterranean Sea and land upon the hammock of the Europe, the continent of economic progress and political culture and stability.

Many, if not all of my chums and co-civil servants knew I would be leaving the Lagoon City of Lagos for Chicago, the windy city. They knew United States would be my destination.

John, (Johnny-come-lately, his nickname) one of my chums, mentioned to me how Europeans, Africans, Asians and South Americans had suffered themselves while contributing to the *greatness* and *mightiness* of America. According to Johnny, all these contributors became heroes of something or something like heroes, for no country in the world has more heroic signatures than America. The encouragements coming from my chums and co-civil servants helped me a lot. Although they did a marvelous thing by encouraging me, many of them were so proud so much that leaving their country more than one month is like losing their oaths of patriotism and dying without marks of identities on their burial grounds.

But like many seekers of overseas education before me, I was contemplating of detouring first to Europe having found it onerous to obtain an American visa in Lagos. Knowing that money is the devil as well as determination of everything, I started saving every naira that was savable.

Nineteen seventy-two came with more determination to leave the country, believing in the saying that traveling is part of education. Sooner than expected, financial help came from my brothers and sisters. They whole-hearted supported the idea of furthering my education as the sole legacy bequeathed to me by Reuben Ojagbuwa Ogunyemi, the lion-hearted Chief of Ipepe. Obviously, and without a nod of denial, all the family members had known by now that their little boy who was not only lucky to be born in a fishing boat but also caused to be born in a fishing vessel while his parents were fishing upon the lagoon, would be leaving his beloved country for another beloved one for good.

By January 1973, my three-year Study Leave Without Pay had been granted and I had begun to give away some of my furniture. According to Chapter 1, page 2, paragraph 3 of the Study Leave, the Federal Government of Nigeria will allow me into its service on finishing my studies.

Consequently, I started visiting and corresponding with the roly-poly princess I thought would be my second half on getting to my destination, as divined by Creator-Philosopher Olodumare. I had commenced to receive prayers of success from prophets, divination philosophers and many visionaries who strongly believe that without God's love and direction, one will stumble and fall. Sometimes, I would fall down on my knees and pray the Author of Life and Death to prepare the way for me, to guide and guard me, to give me the golden fleece so that I could return with honor and credit to my native land amidst the extendedness of our family structure.

July 1973 could not wait for me to give me a count of thirty-one days. Or was it me who could not wait for the end of July before boarding an Alitalia on a beautiful afternoon, the 29th of July, 1973? A day prior to this, brothers and friends had taken "a safe journey photograph" with me. Well-wishes rained upon me like confetti and flakes. Delectation and goodness became my lot. I felt like an emissary going to recover all the mineral wealth and artifacts borrowed during colonization and slavery. There was a dazzling glow upon my countenance.

No sooner the plastic bird took off at the Lagos International Airport (now Murtala International Airport) than I was overwhelmed by evocative emotions. Looking down through my window, I could not restrain my evocative emotions and I did not know when I opened my mouth and commenced the following: Oh beautiful Lagos, capital of the littoral towns and villages, I am leaving you behind inside this aluminum plastic bird. Oh Ipepe, the miracle town and its miracle church, when shall I see you again? What is this new technology doing to me—without my father and my mother—risking my life in a situation in which I could perish like a housefly should an ill-luck strike? Am I going on an exile? Or is it an exile exciting me? Why should I have to go far away from my native home when I can see, hear, touch, smell, feel, taste here almost everything I can see, hear, touch, smell, feel, taste yonder—at the back of beyond? My eyes welled up with tears. My brand new trousers were soaked with tears. I began to sob. I don't think I remember when a flight attendant came to give me a kerchief to wipe my drenched face. I wiped my face but it was never dry.

About an hour before we reached Fiumicino International Airport in Rome, (now Leonardo da Vinci International Airport), I began to accuse Oshun, Oya and Yemoja for not allowing me to become a professional fisher like my brothers. Blaming the goddesses, I asked them why I should suffer: why they should punish me—leaving my parents, my brothers and sisters, my friends and acquaintances, and my roly-poly would-be princess, together with all those macrobiotic things I had sipped and munched such as the succulent fruits, the mouth-watering roe of tilapia and the prize fish—and entering into a shock of another culture whose day and night are unknown to me. I railed at them for being unsympathetic to my destiny, delivering me, a stripling, into the shackles of a twentieth century slavery—a double-edged—self-made vassal.

So much about these tearful evocative emotions: I can take them no more. May the simoom blow them away from the depth of my stomach. Ere the simoom blew them away, I accepted the fact that I had been tied to a plinth and flung in a world of emotionalism, swaying up and down like a seesaw; sometimes, in a merry-go-round like a roulette. I have allowed, by way of omission and commission incidents to emotionalize me, turning me into a shipwrecked emotionalist. Will there be, can there be an empathist, ready to share a modicum of my emotions?

This is no maudlin. No matter how sentimental I was, this is no maudlin at all, for I drank neither sarsaparilla nor palm wine.

Chapter Seventeen

Learning to Become an Italian

Having spent a day and a night in a five-star hotel in Rome, Rome where the destiny of the civilized world was couched for centuries, a hotel which I had wrongly chosen, I was advised to leave for Perugia, by a fellow African. Perugia is the capital of Umbria in the southern part of Italy. The reason why I was advised to leave for Perugia is that there was a colony of Africans there which had solidified itself into an African Students' Union. Added to this fact is the presence of an Italian University for foreigners where foreigners have the opportunities to learn the Italian language.

My dwelling in Perugia was an African House given to the African Students' Union by a Samaritan in the name of Signora Maria. Also living in the same house is my cousin, Adeola Ogunfemi whose invitation after staying in Italy for six months brought me to Italy. Both of us mooned together, shopped together, dined together, reminisced together like identical twins.

My first observation was as open as my palms to other students. I observed that there is no outage. Consequently, I wrote a short letter to the Daily Times in Lagos asking the electricians working with the Nigerian Electric Port Authority (NEPA) to make outages in Nigeria history, adding that if Italians could make their electric power stable, Nigerians could also do likewise.

One day, I looked through my window and saw that it was snowing—light and accumulating. It happened to be my first time of witnessing this heavenly phenomenon. Soon, pondering took hold of me. I pondered and pondered in absolute loneliness. A few hours later, I turned on the television and saw people skiing and jumping. Some broke their necks. Some broke their limbs. Some were carried on stretchers (half-dead than

97

alive) on their way to the hospital. A veil of sympathy enveloped me but that did not stop me from saying and that there are many other ways in which people resort to killing themselves in absence of a natural death.

In the evening, I commenced to relish the highs and lows of the day. But on seeing snow everywhere on the ground, my pondering resumed again. I pondered and pondered until I asked myself why people should call themselves as "white" as snow.

On Adeola's advice, I registered to learn Italian at the Italian University for foreigners. I attended classes two or three times. And that was all. One day, Professor Vinci met me at the plaza and asked me why I had resolved not to attend his language class. I told him that my personal scholarship was not meant for a language studies, adding that if I should have anything more than scholarship, I would channel it toward what would be useful to my country, still on the laps of development.

On the forth month of my arrival in Italy, there was an air of economic nervousness in Europe and America. The cause for this nervousness happened on October 17, 1973 when the Organization of Arab Petroleum Exporting Countries, announced as a result of the on-going Yom Kippur War, that they would no longer ship petroleum to the nations that had supported Israel in its war with Syria and Egypt. What a coincidence? Whether this was a good omen for me or not, there is no way I could verify. All I could verify is that Nigeria was not a party to the embargo, for she badly needs oil money in her bid to develop all the infrastructures and make the land the most modern country in Africa.

After a stay of three months, I discovered a Briton selling some of the popular Italian authors. In other words, he had a mobile bookshop. At this time, Adeola was preparing to go to Vienna in search of a summer job. The Briton invited me to Rome and after a brief interview, he said I was qualified to be part and parcel of his sales team. I don't know what qualified me to be a sales person, however, I gladly accepted his offer and joined his team in a mobile bookshop. We were four altogether:

an Ethiopian, an American, a British and a Nigerian. Our conveyance was an eight-seater van that ensured our mobility from one place to another—we were always on the trot—selling the books to anyone who wanted to buy them as a way to support us—as students. I enjoyed such mobility, the first time I would be in such a mobile bookshop going from one town to another—as far away as Palermo in Sicily. In order to become a good salesperson, I had a few days training in salesmanship. I also improved my Italian language. Conversationally, I improved from day to day.

One beautiful afternoon in Palermo, I sat down on a bench in a park, not far from the shoreline of the Mediterranean Sea, rest-curing myself. Soon I began reminiscing about Olodumare and all his nonpareil creations. I reminisced about the beautiful flowering plants, about the dutiful heavenly bodies—the sun, the moon, the Milky Way and the galaxy of stars, each obeying the law of creation without fail. I reminisced about the seas and the oceans, about the rainy and the dry seasons I was leaving behind and the readiness of my skin for the erratic behaviors of the summer, the autumn, the winter and the spring seasons. I reminisced about the imaginary pendulum of the immortality around my neck and the picturesque serenity during my formative years. With due respect to God and his omnipotence, omnipresence, omniscience, I began to question the rationale behind the existence of the Devil/Satan (in this wonderful and wondrous earth) who has promised to torture, kill and throw asunder every damn good thing Olodumare has created with unsurpassable love and happiness. Death with Satan, Satan with Death: what is the purpose of your existence? No sooner did I ask the question than a young Indian man appeared from my back. He greeted me. I greeted him. On asking me why my life was enriched with friendship, I said, "In the beginning, I started to make friends for Mother told me that making friends is making life. Thus I made so many that I did not regret having so many useful ideas by making friends. Thus I make life. I am part of that life. Life, I am—in me, life, there is—a glowing exuberance."

After conversing for about seven minutes, and exchanged addresses, he asked me to show him my palms. I showed him both palms. He examined both, paying more attention to the lines, and then said to me that I would be a centenarian, living up to one hundred years before I paid my debt to nature. In addition, he said my gourd would be filled with honey by many princesses in my life. No sooner he said this, than he rose and left. When it occurred to me that I should have asked him what he meant by saying that my bottle would be filled with honey by many princesses, I stood up and started looking for him. But he had disappeared without a trace like a miracle and I never see him or hear from him till today.

Three months were not enough to know Italy and her art treasures. But three months were enough to work with the mobile bookshop. Thus I left my mobile job after three months with the hope of going to Vienna, the prepossessing capital of Austria.

Chapter Eighteen

Learning to Become an Austrian

I got to Vienna by train from Perugia at the outset of the Spring-time in 1974. The aurora had begun to blow a whistle of love for the spring-lovers. The insects were chirping. The redstarts were singing. But their melody was coarse, and indeed cacophonous. It could not in any fashion be compared to the melody of the redstart I saw by the brook in 1955. It appears the miasma, caused by pollution, in Austria in general and in Europe in particular, is twisting and damaging the throats of the songbirds. They are losing their natural gift, alas.

In addition to the melody of the redstarts, the flowers had produced their buds, trying to open. Some had opened as a matter of fact. I quickly wrote a letter to thank Signora Maria for her motherly love and generosity. After the letter, I couched the following poem:

Where was your presence?
Where were you?
When the time
Was timing me out to leave?
Are you ready to take the plunge?
Are you ready to leave behind you?
And join me in a world like ours
Created by God?
Let my soul yield some dividend
Let my love wait forever no more.

This poem is short but it means a lot to me. For it was meant for the first princess I was planning to have as my second half. She received the poem but declined to reply. Her silence over my poem shows that she had no interest to join me and subdue me with her passion and the charm of her princess-likeness.

Behaving like Johnny-come-lately, without being told, I was left to do battle with loneliness. As soon as it was defeated, I sent a message home to my relatives to find on my behalf another gorgeous princess. In no time at all, a gorgeous new princess was found and correspondences started in earnest. Her letters were encouraging as they were romantic. To confirm the seriousness of her love, she sent to me a pair of dashikis which were of value to me during the sweltering summer days. I was proud of her love. But as days rolled over days and months rolled over months, that pride started to dwindle. This time I was a victim of a new taste provided by a Vienna princess. Her name is Silvia Hrusa.

Before the end of 1974, Trans-Continental Poems was completed. It is a book that portrays my evocative emotions as I left behind everything except immortality I have known, and read about Nigeria and consuming little by little everything about Europe. One thing is certain about the book. It is certain that I could not have written the book without the phrasal thought of **Reading is Good. Writing is Creative** which I have carried from Nigeria with the courtesies of Jedo and Priscilla, respectively.

In 1975, I completed a Diploma Program in Journalism by Distance Learning at the London School of Journalism. This was the year I met my first girlfriend, Silvia Hrusa, a law student at Vienna University, one of the oldest universities in central Europe. A diligent and well-informed student, Silvia and her parents supported me in gaining my foothold in Vienna. I owe them many words of gratitude. They taught me German which the stubbornness in my head refused to grasp. The reason is that my head wanted nothing less than English which my head had been familiar with since my salad days. And I made this known to one and all that every student coming from a developing country should make use of the *developed language* which he/she had been using before leaving his/her developing country.

Silvia and I visited many interesting places in Vienna. One of such places of interest is Schoenbrunn where Maria Theresa (1717-1780), Holy Roman Empress, Archduchess of Austria, Queen of Hungary and Bohemia. The Austrian history shows that she was the eldest daughter of Charles VI who promulgated the Pragmatic Sanction to allow her to succeed to the Habsburg monarchy. Opposition to the throne led to the War of the Austrian Succession in 1740.

A pragmatic empress, Maria Theresa helped initiate financial and educational reforms. She promoted commerce and the development of agriculture, and reorganized the army, thus strengthening Austria's resources. She was a prominent figure in the power politics of 18th century Europe. She brought unity to the quarrelsome Habsburgs Monarchy and was considered one of its most capable rulers. I was however, taken aback on learning that she gave birth to sixteen children, making me believe that she was not only a strong being of motherhood but also one of the few women in the world to give birth to sixteen children at her time without losing anyone of them at infancy.

Another place Silvia and I visited whose history made my hair stand on end is the Spanish Riding School, at the court of Hofburg in central Vienna. Here the horses known as the Lipizzaners represent the pinnacle of equestrian performance. The white horses, oh they are great. How they prance about on their tiptoes made me think they are trained like magicians.

I did not know exactly how many times Silvia and I went for a dip. I guess it should not be less than three times. One of such dips which I will never forget until I pay my debt to nature is when I nearly drowned. This happened during a seductive summer day. The sky was sky-blue and romantic. The sun was glowing perpendicularly above, producing a kind of heat that sent many people maddening about. At the same time, there was a kind of breeze that produced comfortableness, especially under a shade. I remember telling Silvia that the city of Vienna was enjoying nature's dual hospitality.

It took us less than two hours on a public transportation before getting to a man-made lake at the outskirts of the city. We strode into the clean open-air site, hand in hand like a royal couple. There were a few jealous glances, darted at us but the tangent was maintained. Nothing went at it. Hundreds of people had been dipping and tanning their skins before we got there. The question at the depth of my stomach is: why should I tan my skin after exposing it conditionally and tropically for over twenty memorable years? But as luck would have it, we managed to find a poky place, not far away from the shade of a bunya-bunya-like sycamore.

While stretching our limbs under the dappled shade of the sycamore, I honored Silvia with two poems, indited hastily with the affection in the air. They are: Travel in a Friendship Boat and Romance & Love.

Travel in a Friendship Boat:
My heart dismayed
Seeing the river rough, wild, wild.

But gently you held my hand
And together we entered, seated
And started rowing in unison.

Sooner than expected
My dismal evaporated
As the river calmed
Shimmering and enchanting.

You looked into my eyes and said
"It's because we are friends,
Our friendship has lulled
The rough, wild, wild river to calm."

Slowly the currents carried our boat
From Darling Island to Honey Island

104

As we landed, you said
Friendship with Understanding
With one heart, the primary medicine.

Swallowing it, it becomes
A cure-all
I acquiesced with a winsome smile
As big as the full moon
Beaming above our heads.

Romance & Passion
Befriend me, first
Understanding, a second phenomenon
Then love and romance
Tied with compromise and tolerance
A foundation of a house.

In a stormy day
Spring, summer, fall or winter
The house will stand
The test of time.

For a house built
With friendship and love
Walled with understanding
Stands forever!

Subsequently, we approached the lake whose waves were like the ripples of smiles among the pampas and veld when it was not motorized. In no time at all, my friend displayed to me her prowess to swim like a turtle and lay afloat like a cork. I was impressed much as I was stupefied with amazement.

In a spirit of competition, I told her that I could swim as she had done. Almost effortlessly, I swam just as she had done. Also, she was impressed much as she was stung by an imaginary bee, forcing her mouth into an ugly shape that could be described as agape.

Respectively, both of us are good swimmers even if the level of our knowledge is beneath that of an amateur. Let me confess. I must confess that when it comes to backstroke and butterfly, Silvia could easily become my instructor without recommendation. She could beat the Commonwealth Australian female Gold medalist swimmer to the first place if the latter is not wary enough. She is good. The credit of being good is hers.

DROWNING BY CHOICE: As both of us were enjoying ourselves, lying down under the bunya-bunya-like sycamore, I decided to take another dip into the middle of the lake where the waves were brutally violent. First, I started to enjoy myself— swimming effortlessly. Later, I began to encounter some *wahala* in that the waves were pushing hard against me as I was swimming toward the bank. It was like racing against the wind. Those waves could hardly be noticed were they in a sea. But here, inside this man-made lake, their rolling force could be matched with tsunamis.

After five minutes, I noticed that the strength in my arms was diametrically gone. Then I struggled to let my feet touch the floor of the lake. Yes, my feet got there but my head was under water to do this. However, I forced myself to walk with my head submerged but I could not. The currents and the waves did not permit me to do this. It was my first-time experience that human beings are not made to walk under water, not when we are not aquatics or aquatic monsters!

All this time, my friend, Silvia was under the illusion that I was relishing myself as she lay under the sycamore waiting for me, not knowing that I was fighting tooth and nail for my survival. She did not know that I was drowning! I imagined Death and its agents pulling my legs into the void and Life and its angels pulling me out of the void.

All of a sudden: when least expected, my feet began to flirt with the floor of the lake. At the same time, I noticed that the waves had lost their strength to drag me back into the swirl of their force, and the Death vanished. On reaching the bank, and lying half-dead than alive, I commenced muttering to my friend that Oshun, through the grace of Olodumare must have saved my life from drowning. She pursed in disbelief. She held me by hand and I stood up thanking Olorun for saving my life. That is the last time I enjoyed a sunny summer day by swimming.

From all accounts as evidenced by what I did to survive, my journalistic training enabled me to work with the World of Diplomats and the Vienna News from 1976 to 1977as a reporter. Working with those two news magazines enabled me to know many Vienna diplomats. Interviewing all those international diplomats and having cocktails with them made me feel not only like a diplomat but also made me feel at the top of the world. My debonair and countervailing laissez faire nearly made me attend the prestigious Vienna Diplomatic School and on finishing my training, become an ambassador at large.

Chapter Nineteen

The Death of a Reporter

THE DEMISE OF A REPORTER: In 1976, as my association with the Vienna News became cordial and things swimming smoothly in my favor, three policemen invaded my apartment and whisked me away. It was a Tuesday late afternoon. I saw their van packed almost opposite the entrance door to my apartment as I was coming from the British Council Library where I had been burying my head in books authored by Commonwealth men and women but had no inkling that they were waiting in ambush for me. Not quite five minutes I entered my apartment, they pounced one me. The ambush was led by a pot-beer-bellied commander with a domed forehead. It bears no harm to compare his forehead with a Nigerian minister in the 1980s who was caught at the airport carrying in his brief-case one million in various currencies— dollars, pounds, Deutsch-marks and yens. My veniality was that I had no visa in my passport. They also accused me of tergiversation for saying to the editor-in-chief of the Vienna News that I did not know whether to stay put in Austria or to go to America for further studies. If ever I made a conflicting statement, it was because I was boxed in by shilly-shally. How did they know that my visa had expired? How did they find out where I was living? I could suspect only my editor-in-chief—to have stabbed me in the back despite our cordial working relationship, he should be accused of malversation. He had violated one of the fundamental values of journalism which asks every journalist to protect his/her own. This fine figure of a journalist, a podgy man who will find it difficult to escape through my poky kitchen window would often tell me that what the Vienna News was paying me was too little as to enjoy myself fully in the beautiful city of Vienna. Sometimes he would tell me to ask my embassy to employ me. "A brilliant reporter like you should be employed by your embassy since they don't have a journalist of their own." My finger, as well as other fingers, on hearing my own side of the tale, thus point to Manfred or was it Neumayer, I couldn't remember the true cognomen of the traitor in his gentlemanliness. For sure, he is not Dr. Walther E. Ullmann, the respected editor of the "World of Diplomats." Now I remember the gentleman's name. He is Kurt Frischler.

First, I was locked up in a windowless detention room that looks very much like a garret or snuggery. The following day, I was interrogated by the Vienna detectives who wanted to know why a journalist did not have a visa in his passport. My reply was simple. My passport needed a renewal from the Nigerian Embassy. A few hours after the interrogation, I was taken to a non-criminal underground clink where I saw other law breakers, mostly Turks, overstaying their welcomes.

For the first twenty-four hours, I did not know what to say or what to do. I was somehow deflated—simply gawping and gawking. Loss of appetite had started to show some signs on my tongue. I was sick and tired of munching the popular goulash, simply because it was too salty for my taste bud. Apart from the vegetables, the only meal that always made me bite my tongue is Vienna schnitzel—invariably well-prepared and topped with the Polish or Irish mashed potatoes. Vienna (Wiener) schnitzel, a breaded, garnished and fried veal, is a mouth-watering schnitzel. Eating it often makes my eyes shed tears of joy but its gusto could not be compared in any shred of imagination to those tilapia's hard roe, relished tongue-bitingly during the age of innocence. If one day I choose to become a gourmet, I would remember how palatable the tilapia's hard roe was even if it is at the doorstep of the Pearly Gates.

Much, so much, now depended on how my friends and my nodding acquaintances in the free world would talk about me, gossipingly. The journalistic five questions, predicated upon where, when, who, how and why would be the talks of the town—on their lips—gossipingly. Some of their gossips would or could be, "Poor Yemi, he is in a clink and he could only see the free world through a chink. If this kind of gossip should ramify across the borders and land on my mother's laps, the sad news would cripple her, for her son will be the first human being in the family to be suffering under the lock whereas I should be enjoying the good and humble name of the family in peace, love, happiness and abundant good health. "Should this happen, would she comprehend the whys and the wherefores? Is this the whirli-gig of time?" I would ask myself. Sometimes, I felt like whining, knowing that all my friends and acquaintances are enjoying a full fledged freedom, while I was gawking and yawping in an underground lock-up. I had begun to reflect upon how my life had moved from sublime to bathos, and how I would fight tooth and nail to move it from bathos to sublime.

On the second day, my reflection was totally on writing. I started to wonder whether I would ever utter, "Reading is good, writing is creative." Without a book, a journal, sheets of paper and a typewriter in my possession, it seemed I had lost the cultural oasis of my mind. Life could be wasted doing nothing, I thought.

As my loneliness metamorphosed into disorientation and vice versa, my imagination began to assume a wider dimension. As a matter of fact, I was on a merry-go-round of imagination. And I swear if I did know when I proceeded to flay the world for the harm it must have done to its citizens who must have spent a year or more in a lonely confinement like mine. I accused the world so much that brutality appeared like a ghoul in my imagination and commenced to torment the officer on duty.

It was my curvaceous girlfriend, Silvia who discovered that the law had tampered with my freedom. How did she know that I had been smuggled from the light to the darkness? Soon after I was brought to the underground confinement, I was asked to fill out a form and to indicate who to be contacted in a situation such as this. I wrote down Silvia's name and her telephone number. Minutes later, Silvia was alerted by Rudolf, a kindhearted policeman on duty and Silvia in a crying voice

111

informed my embassy that I had been kidnapped by the law enforcers and put in a detention for the second day running. That very day, Silvia and Yellow, an embassy diplomat, and a friend of mine, visited me in my den of loneliness. I was flushed with joy to receive them. With Silvia's kiss, small but mighty for the occasion, I was resuscitated and glowing with passion— completely resuscitated but feeling ill at ease.

On securing my release from this all-consuming imagination, I tearfully longed for *The Man Died,* a book by Wole Soyinka, published in 1972, written when he was incarcerated from 1967 to 1969. Putting myself in Wole's position, I blubbered and wondered whether my situation would force me, torment me so much that I would have the luxury to become the second wordsmith in Nigeria to scribble a prison memoir to be entitled *The Man Died,* whose subtitle should be *The Demise of a Journalist.*

Rudolf, the young weedy and ambidextrous police officer on duty, always portrays an attitude that characterizes affability and admixture of eastern and western practicality. His father, a Czech Jew, escaped the torture and the bloody sledgehammer of Nazism but his grandfather was not so lucky. He was one of the many who perished during Hitler's totalitarian leadership as Fuhrer from 1934 to 1945 which resulted in the killing of over six million Jews in Holocaust.

Born in Vienna in 1954, Rudolf did not like to work in an underground place like this. He was unhappy man who invariably found his happiness by chatting with us—the law-breaking foreigners who were relishing their punishment in the underground detention. Still regarding himself an accidental citizen of Austria, he had promised to help us overcome the pangs of our loneliness by chatting with us. One or two times, I cannot guarantee the number of times, Rudolf would prevail on me to munch the salty goulash. And in absence of my delicious schnitzel, I would force myself to have the salty meal to fill my empty stomach even if my gorge rises at seeing it.

Added to his affability, he would let us know that he always said something good about us whenever his higher-up came to inspect our situation. Most of the time, I kept my lips tight. I did not tell him why I was mealy-mouthed even if he had asked me several times if I was not enjoying the company of my co-detainees. It was an honorable thing to be mealy-mouthed after my experience with my former podgy editor-in-chief, for once bitten, twice shy.

The entire seven days in a week passed, there was no charge pressed against me. As the second week was maturing to an end, I got hold of a rough piece of paper loaned to me by my girlfriend and scribbled my concerns to Dr. Bruno Kreisky, the chancellor of Austria. Within a short period of time, I was released and my embassy was adjured to issue me a brand new passport. Silvia, my inamorata and my friendly embassy diplomat, Mr. Yellow, quickly ensured the availability of the new passport. Thereafter, I learn how to protect my passport, jealously, knowing full well that this government document is more important than money when it comes to traveling from one border to another.

Silvia was a little bit bitter with me on reaching my apartment. The reason is that I had told her during the course of our friendship that a prince like me needs no visa in his passport wherever he goes. I said this, as a real prince, in order to sweeten her imagination, for it was made known to me that most European girls/ladies prefer boys/men of substance to fall in love with. On knowing that the police had arrested me for not having a visa in my passport, she then regarded my story as a lie, questioning the contents of my character. But I was not the only one in the crowd. There were other boys who would sugar-coat their lips by saying that their fathers were oil moguls, importers and exporters of gold and diamonds, handlers of ivory tusks, boutique owners, diplomats, emperors, jackpot hitters, inheritors of the family wealth, ship-builders, owners of tankers, presidents, cocoa farm-owners, cassava farm-owners, groundnut planters, exporters of coffees, launderers whose booties were stashed away in Swiss banks. Yet others sweetened the imaginations of their girlfriends by saying that they were holders of UN laissez-passers.

To cut a long story short, I flopped on my knees and prayed Silvia to forgive my acting, adding that it was the smoke that betrayed the fire. On promising her that I would never, never act falsely again, she said munificently that I need to comprehend that love goes in tandem with honesty, adding that a true love/friend heals like a story from a honest mouth. I could not agree less.

After writing a heart-warming letter to Dr. Bruno Kreisky, thanking him for prompting my release, I went back to the office of the Vienna News, and the podgy editor-in-chief was jiggered, even scared to see me. His pupils dilated and his lips trembled. He could hardly believe his eyes, for he thought I must have been deported to Nigeria after the home police had arrested me and accused me of living and working in the country without a valid visa in my passport. Grinning like a jackpot winner, pouting like a target-loser, and looking askance at him, I stepped out of his journal-crowded office with a chivalrous thank-you-nod that befits a pro-journalist and then flopping into a new surge of air—breezing the rest of my life.

Hurrying out of his office, he met me waiting for the lift. In a voice coated with compunction, he asked, "Where have you been?" This question seemed not to have come from his guided consciousness.

"I have been ensconcing," was my reply. I felt like asking Ogun, the family's deity, the Muse and the artificer of steel and iron, to shower upon him thunderbolts of invectives. To do so is to make him see the rough edge of my tongue, for such a rough edge is a commonplace in Africa. But this is not Africa but Europe and while in Europe I must act like the Europeans.

A few days after my release, Mr. and Mrs. Hrusa, Silvia's parents, invited me to a dinner in their cozy apartment in the Third District—with the courtesy of Silvia. (The city of Vienna

114

is partitioned into twenty-three districts.) The dinner, in a congenial atmosphere like a cozy restaurant, was sumptuous, and Wiener schnitzel was not missing. As a matter of fact, it was the most delicious menu I could recollect with a slapping grin and a sweet-sounding guffaw.

After the dinner, I seized the opportunity to intimate Silvia and her parents with the full-fledged story of the Yoruba people. Summarizing it, I said, "The Yoruba people occupy the southwest of Nigeria and they can be found in other West African countries such as the republic of Benin, Togo and Ghana. With over twenty million, as it were in the 1970s: now close to forty million, they are the largest ethnic group in Nigeria.

"They are noted for their city-states. The most notable and perhaps the largest of all are the Ile-Ife and Oyo kingdoms. The biggest indigenous city in Africa today is Ibadan whose ground upholds and initiates the first University in Nigeria.

"Ifa Divination which is otherwise known as the Book of Enlightenment is one of the oldest systems of worship in the world. In other words, the indigenous religion is Ifa Divination which obligates the scions of the land to worship Creator-Philosopher Olodumare (God) through his messengers, the Orisas. Today, many Yoruba people have embraced Islam and Christianity as their new-found religions.

"The Yoruba artistic works are unique. They include weaving, beadwork, metalwork, mask-making and terra-cottas. Most of their artworks are made to honor the ancestors and Oisas who are over 400 in number, making Yoruba to be compared to ancient Greece in the amount of gods and goddesses. The Yoruba religion is the most popular religion among the Africans living outside of Africa.

"Oduduwa is the founder and the king of the Yoruba people and every ruler in Yorubaland is dynastically attached to him. That is why every Yoruba person has a royal blood in him/her. He or she is blue-blooded. That is why I can confidently call myself a prince, albeit insignificant.

"Comparatively, Ifa Divination is like the Bible to the ancient Yoruba. That is why it is being referred to as the Book of Enlightenment. And every humble Yoruba man or woman has to know a little bit of it because it is the metaphysical concept central to Yoruba philosophy, religion and literature."

Father, Mother and Daughter heaved a sigh of relief on finishing my short account on the Yoruba people. Their faces were aglow, wreathed in smiles that nearly made me whine. In unison, they said I had taken them to Nigeria as a result of my lecture and that they see find no reason to visit the country any longer.

Having told them about the python that the Almighty God prevented from swallowing me whole in 1959 and the fire that nearly burnt me to ashes in 1956, and my two weeks' experience in the underground detention, I let them know that what has happened and would happen to me is an integral part of the vicissitudes of life which also could be juxtaposed with the whirli-gig of time, adding (from the rest-cure of my mind) that I had mistakenly borrowed trouble while trouble was ensconcing in a stygian corner without a stir.

Father and Mother wanted to know why on earth I should choose to come to Austria. They told me (as their daughter, Silvia had) that life could be difficult in a non-English-speaking country like Austria.

Asked if my landlord was treating me well, my answer was a monosyllabic yes. Furthermore, I told them that my landlord was treating me like a princely gentleman. They smiled even if they were swallowed by bewilderment because Silvia had given me the gist that Austria is one of the European countries which had conservatively distorted the image of Africa. I have no idea until then that Europeans have regarded Africans as inferior to them, skinning them with unholy misnomers in spite of the fact that every European household owns a Holy Bible. Why is it that human beings are so negative of others in their thoughts? Why is it that the Holy Bible does not serve as the guide and guidance in our everyday life? I could not comprehend the whys and

116

wherefores. I think I was still being tossed up and down and left and right between naivety and sheer innocence.

In order to let them know that their fear was not diametrically baseless, I reminded them of the dramatic telephone conversation betwixt a London landlady and Wole Soyinka in the 1960s. Wole found it difficult to secure an apartment to rent in London in 1962 just because of his God-given skin-color, a blue-blooded man from Africa. Alas, what happened to Africans during the days of un-civilization is still happening today. Is history repeating itself? How far away is civilization? Dead in Europe, resurrecting in Africa? Is civilization born already or is it a scrap? There are numerous questions sans answers.

It was around 9 pm by the time I got to my apartment in the sixth district. The above questions remained unanswered before I kipped down. Listening to the voice of my alter ego, he said that I had had a successful day because I have been able to put smiles on the faces of other people—three people. I prayed and thanked the Lord, joyfully. I went to bed, joyfully. I slept, joyfully. I dreamt, joyfully. And I woke up in the morn, joyfully and peacefully, glorifying and worshipping the Lord that I have been able to spend a day, joyfully and peacefully—through his grace.

I was so happy to learn that my historic letter to Chancellor Bruno Kreisky and my eventual release did lead to the release of more than ten of the detainees—one after the other. Ayuk, a young Turkish student, with whom I often conversed in English in lieu of German, ran into me two moons later and broke the news that because I had made the incommunicable to be communicated, and then opened the door, other detainees had no other choice but to go through and breathe the air of freedom. We confabulated for more than three hours, regaling on our cups of cappuccinos in between, criticizing the police for detaining us without trial. Deporting a law breaker to his/her home country is the logical thing to do but not to detain him/her indefinitely—in a dungeon.

Mobility is the universal story of being alive and kicking. Wherever one's mobility is hindered, one's inalienable right is likely to be in jeopardy. In sum and substance, my release was a timely defense of reason, justice, transparency and seminality.

TELEPHONE DIALOGUE: (Betwixt Silvia and Yemi three days after visiting her and her parents: three days after that unforgettable slap-up dinner):

Silvia: As a man with eclectic views, how do you want me to help you? The problems in Africa are so complex that each and every one of you has to play an increasingly constructive role.

Yemi: This is true, Silvia. But I guess there are hunger and political problems in Africa because of one thing.

Silvia: What is that one thing?

Yemi: I don't want to mention this because people may not take it serious. If I should say it, it is because I love your country as a land that believes in God, the Creator of all peoples.

Silvia: Please tell me what you have in mind.

Yemi: It is because of Apartheid, often referred to as poli-eco-social problems or injustice.

Silvia: Expatiate on this poli-eco-social theory.

Yemi: The African countries should stop accepting development aid. The givers of development aid should first of all strangle Apartheid.

Silvia: What follows then?

Yemi: What follows then is the civilization of the 20th century if you want me to put it that way. As at now development aid is like a replacement for Apartheid.

Silvia: Do you mean that there should be no technical aid? Do you mean the poor people in Africa should be left to die of hunger?

Yemi: They die of hunger because of Apartheid. The more the African countries receive development aid, the more they indirectly support Apartheid.

Silvia: It is very hard to believe this theory of yours, Yemi.

Yemi: I know. But let me disclose to you that it is a psychological, political and economical vicious circle which givers of development aid continue to follow. Hunger is one thing but it is more honorable for mankind to *die of hunger* than to be *burnt alive*—just because of racial discrimination, which is apartheid policy.

Silvia: An end to Apartheid will come one day! And when that day comes, it will be a new era of modern civilization since the end of the 2nd World War and a badge of Excellence for the United Nations.

Yemi: This generation needs such a peaceful, paradise-like civilization.

Silvia: One day, *enough* shall be *enough* for the South Africa—where all colors of people will live side by side with each other.

From 1979 to 1980, I was appointed correspondent for the African interpreters, based in Bonn, Germany. The news magazine was not popular in Austria but it was in Germany.

Between 1977 and 1979, I was a Communications student at the University of Graz which is about two hundred kilometers south of Vienna. This was after I had spent about eight months at Vienna University of Dramatic Art, Film and Television, 1976-1977. Although I did not complete the one-year program, I gained some useful knowledge regarding dramaturgy, film and television.

Chapter Twenty

Fatherhood

THE NATURAL BLESSING: Oh gosh: oh Jesus of Nazareth, my feeling was ethereal. It was great to own the key of paternity. It was indeed palpable. It an extraordinary feeling, and I could feel my blood coursing the veins from head to toe. Nothing stops me from equating it with the feeling Joseph had when his wife, Mary gave birth to Messiah in the manger. The feeling of fatherhood, the feeling of being a father, for the first time, in my acquired life of immortality is dramatically indescribable. It was like the feeling one possesses watching the pupa metamorphosing into an imago. Spiritual wellness descended upon me like a spray of holy water. Touching or looking at the stomach of my Love carrying the child who would call me "papa or baba," is a blessed feeling which everyone in my shoes must have experienced, and giving adoration to the King of Kings and the Lord of Lords. This is the all-caressing and all-tickling feeling I had when Maria Rindhauser, a girlfriend of mine, gave birth to a bouncing baby boy—Daniel Adebowale Rindhauser a year prior to the successful completion of my program at the University of Graz. I invited her into marriage but she refused, saying her type is not ideal for a matrimonial home. What she meant by that is not clear to me till this moment. All I know is that she is a daughter of bucolic parents who are very hard-working. In addition to this, she is pretty, humble, diligent and respectable. Only once I speculated the reason she did not want to enjoy a respectable married and a would-be happy life is her addiction to cigarette smoking, for she cannot do without it in a blessed day. She might not smoke when the day is not blessed. I guess you know what I am driving at.

This is the story I narrated to Daniel Adebowale as he was growing up to become a young man. Once upon a time, there was Mother Chick and her chick. They lived in a house built upon a meadow where pecking was forbidden. Because pecking was not allowed, Mother Chick and her chick had to cover some distance before they could find anything to peck.

One day after filling their gizzards to the full, they started on their way home. Soon the sky was overcast, showing a sign that it would rain cats and dogs. So they started to hurry home. At this juncture, a kite, a vulture and an eagle were gliding and swooping up and down, looking for something to prey on. It was the eagle which noticed the presence of Mother Chick and her chick. It started watching them. But was disappointed when the feathered creatures entered their house and began to roost.

As both of them were resting, the chick told her mother that she would like to play outside. Her mother advised her not to do so, adding that there was an enemy outside that was preparing to steal and kill her at anytime. But the chick did not listen, saying that she wanted only to walk around the house for some fresh air.

Unable to persuade her, Mother Chick allowed her to go. No sooner she stepped her feet outside, walking around their house than the eagle swooped down and clawed her. As the bird of prey was carrying her into the sky, Mother Chick heard the cry of her chick for help. She rushed out of the house. But it was too late. The eagle had found its prey as a result of disobedience.

During my studies at the University of Graz, I sold many copies of "The Trans-Continental Poems," published by the Institute of African, Asian and Latin-American Studies. I had the opportunities to be invited on a number of occasions by the Junior and High Schools in Graz and Vienna to lecture on Nigerian/African literatures, and to read from the poetry book. It was another memory of feeling good.

In the spring of 1978, I sent a copy of "The Trans-Continental Poems" to the Federal Ministry of Information in

Lagos, requesting the Director of Information to publish a number of the poems in *Nigeria Illustrated*, the ministry's monthly magazine.

On receiving the booklet, Olu Akinyemi, one of the senior officers of the ministry sent me a praise-worthy letter, dated May 29, 1978, thanking me for showing interest in the ministry's magazine.

In his closing paragraph, he wrote, "You are further congratulated for your aspiration and unflinching love for your fatherland exhibited in most of your poems." My muted hosanna of happiness is that *reading is good, writing is creative.*

On completing my studies in 1979, I came to Vienna. In October of that year, I joined the International Atomic Energy Agency. At this time, a baobab whose leaves were riddled with discrimination, prejudice, ignorance, xenophobia, intolerance and malarkey had just begun to shed its leaves.

Between 1979 and 1982, my parents could not recognize me. Why? It's because I had allowed my life to plunge into a ditch of debauchery. Smoking, drinking alcohol and chasing had become my joie de vivre: my cup of Vienna goulash. In parties and discos, smoking and drinking in the company of my Vienna friends became my new-born social attitude. I was simply following the multitude, not making use of my own faculty. Apparently, I had forgotten how a motor vehicle nearly rolled over me in Ijebu-Ode while playing dangerously with Fola. What a shame! I had not learnt my lesson. A year later, I dreamt and God in his loving-kindness gave me a hand and pulled me out of the pond of debauchery. I was enlightened. Since then, I made smoking and drinking alcohol history.

Unquestionably, credit has to be given to Dr. Bruno Kreisky as a result of the above—the demise of the baobab. He was a respectable Austrian Chancellor who did not want people to refer to him as a Jewish politician but simply as an Austrian politician. Bruno Kreisky was the gentleman who fought tooth and nail to ensure the growth of an international community— UNO in the capital city of Vienna. His dream came true in 1979 when Vienna did not only become an international community of peoples around the world but also was officially declared the United Nations City, coming after New York and Geneva. And Kreisky, a socialist, was seen a victor over the conservative politicians, some of whom had been fanning the embers of xenophobia.

Working with the International Atomic Energy Agency provided many opportunities in Vienna, now an international city of beauty and quaintness. I had a limited immunity, to my delectation. I could travel to anywhere in the world without being rough-handled by the immigration officers.

"Hurrah, Vienna has opened its doors to the world," I said once, twice even thrice as I saw hundreds of people coming to Vienna to work or to live. With the headquarters of the OPEC, more and more peoples from all walks of life were flocking into the city for the meetings in respect of International Atomic Energy Agency (IAEA) or for the meetings in respect of the Organization of Petroleum Exporting Countries (OPEC) or in respect of the peoples coming to attend the annually held Vienna International Opera.

Going around the country, I could notice that the political and the social, as well as the economic face of Austria in general and Vienna in particular changed during this time, for many of the African students, diplomats and business entrepreneurs, especially the Nigerians, brought a new lease of injection into the Vienna music life. Fela Kuti's sound could be heard in almost every weekend party, and in discos. Vienna nightlife changes forever. A novel love has emerged from a stygian corner of the conservative land. A new day has dawned.

Also, here in Austria I saw that people have to fight four times in a year in order to survive, compared to two times I was used to in Nigeria—fighting to survive during the rainy and dry seasons. Here in Austria, during the summer time, the struggle seems to be hectic and less expensive. The spring and the autumn seasons are more hectic and expensive than the summer time. But when the cold winter sets in, the way to survive is the only prayer on the lips—buying the winter paraphernalia, heating the house and keeping oneself warm and healthy costs time and a lot of money. And I was quick to assume why Europeans are richer than Africans who need little or nothing to survive whenever nature compels them to follow its footsteps—two times in a year. As one colleague of mine put it, "I think Africans are richer and at peace with whatever they have, for while a European maybe spending ten dollars on a plate of dinner to satisfy his gorge, an African maybe spending just one dollar on a plate for his own dinner." I could not agree with him less.

Chapter Twenty-One

In Honor of the Visionary
(The President that Never Ruled)

In 1981, I thought it fit to reproduce here, Part One of *Heroic Ballads*, first published in 1974, under the cover of African Soul: Part Two was published in 1986 when the hero died. The drama or any action ends whenever the hero dies. But in the case of this hero who was the president that never ruled, his unfinished action never ends. The torch he lit at the end of the tunnel still glows. And many people continue to wonder why the citizens of his beloved country did not accept his eternal actions while he was alive. Why are they accepting them now? Is it because the time has come to exhume the truth that was once interred?

"Why was he called a hero?" I asked my father.

My father answered, "He was called a hero, a valiant man who never deserted his supporters and went to another country, when his plan was uprooted, because he introduced free primary education to the Western Nigeria. He introduced the first television house in Africa. He improved the status quo of the farmers, as farming was booming, built the Cocoa House, the Liberty Stadium, improved the lot of the sportsmen and women (the Shooting Stars, a glaring example), and made teaching profession worthwhile for the teachers."

Now then, let's peruse the heroic ballads as published in 1986 when the hero decided to join the long line of his pedigrees without being given the chance to complete his mission for the nation.

Measureless signs of time

But the sun has risen
Ne'er to be set again.

The hour has come
The day has dawned
The clock has struck.

The week has come
The moon has phased
The year has come
The clock has chimed.

I still don't comprehend
What my father was
Ruminating about
But he confirmed that
The clock has struck.

"Wait I tell you," said my father.
"What I mean is that
You're too young
To know what's going on.

"Yesterday, I told you
The hour has come
I told you the day
Has dawned
I told you the week
Has come
Told you the moon
Has phased
Told you the year
Has come
But you seemed not to
Understand your father
Because of your tender age?

128

"What I mean is that
A man, a visionary man indeed
A man from a humble family
Has risen like our *sun*
And like the proverbial phoenix."

Wondering, yes I did
Avowed man of vision
Born to say and save.

"He'll build abodes and schools
He'll feed the needy with food and water
He'll clothe the naked
He's the shepherd—the Je-Messiah."

"How can I understand you, father when
You keep me in darkling suspense
Fenced by shilly-shally?"

"Fated child, in search of a nimble mind
How can you understand
When you're too young to see?"

"But I know the clock
Has struck
The day has dawned
With iridescence.

"I have dreamed about him
Even before he was fated
To feed the hungry.

"Watch out:
Your eyes, shall new things behold
Your ears shall hear new things
Your nose will smell a new scent of life

Your limbs shall touch and feel
Your tongue shall taste
The impact of his fated intentions
For this land, for you and I
For he changed his academic law into
The law of productivity of our natural resources."

I waited the whole 1954
Impatient, breathing
The scent of a new change in the country.

Conditioned by history
Overpowered by aliens
I know the country in the hands of
The colonial soothsayers and pseudo-philosophers
Destined to be free: must be free.

Even then, nothing was unequivocal
but my father swore by the name
Of our kitchen god, the fire, that
Independence has been scribbled in
The palpable air
To be breathed in
Mattered, measured no more than
Forty winks.

But my father was telling me
A narrative more anecdotal than
The wombed Independence
A narrative tagged as the power of pen
Does one traditionally disbelieve
An elderly man,
A Chief for that matter?

No. May 1955 bring that new Messiah
Was my supplication

As I slept from 1954 to 1955. I saw my father as the door of
my supplication closed with Amen—Ase.
The reason to know
What he prophesied
The previous year
Was a-new in my head.
He did hesitate to let me
Know that he would lead me
To the same fairy land of suspense
Yes, God of mercy, I opened my eyes—thankfully
I strained my ears
Rejoicing in the wisdom
Of an Elder.

"Now the year has come
The clock has struck," he repeated
As he used to say.
"Now I shall hold you by hand
And lead you out
Of the fairy land of suspense
The visionary man
The world is talking about is
Philosopher Obafemi Awolowo."

"Is he ready to feed the nation?"

"Yes, he is the sole soul, vowed to do just that,
Selflessly, truthfully."

Memories die never too soon
Supporting the living, truths in a man
May these memories kindle a spirit
Of Love, devotion, in you and me
I supplicated, selflessly.

Years of moiling and toiling
The burden and heat of the day
The burden and heat of the night
From it comes a true lover of this country.

As my father reaffirmed:
No year, no history shall ever be without
This year! This fateful, this blessed year!
Because you and I shall pay
No fees for our education!

Again, I asked my father: "How much will the nation pay
him?"

"He demands nothing, bribes no one."

"But how could he sacrifice his energy for me when I don't
him?"

"You will know him, today and forever
His patriotic soul, his humanitarian mind
A nationalist
A redeemer
Anti-materialism."

Could we offer him
A gourd of palm wine or a jug of sarsaparilla?

"No he drinks no alcohol."

"Could we present him with some cigars?"

"No he never smokes
Never, always a teetotaler
Supporting all
But opposing Nigeria, richer than Nigerians

He is a modest gentleman."
A modest gentleman?
I repeated to myself
May we all be modest
And leave the surpluses
For the needy and yet-to-be born—capital AMEN.

To the backyard, I went
And wept for joy
The smoke belching out from
The backyard door
Cocking my eyes
Intensifying my weeping—joyfully.

The days of uncertainties
Are gone, gone forever.

The peace to read and write
Came like the healing raindrops upon my head

Matched with the anticipated
Peace of my father's piscatorial culture.

When I slept
A supplication opened

My heart and said
May the sons and daughters of this
Unevenly created fingers of hand

Recognize and give him
A chance to save them all.

Chance betrayed
Politics betrayed, degraded
Eternal truths crushed, yoked

Darkness surged, darker than cumulus,
More terrifying than anarchies
Later, reality, a dawn
Belated, however
But after the terrifying darkness
On the horizon, the sun rises
But again, betrayal, eternal truths again, crushed.

Now he sleeps, embracing the eternal truths
Glued with serendipity
His Holy Sepulcher policed
By the angels whose lips were wedged open by dirges
Signaled his eternal love for the needy and for his country.

Even in his grave
My father will continue to thank him
By saying, many wars could have been
Without you
Many wrongs could have been
Without you
Many illiteracies could have been
Without you.

That long-kindled torch of vision and the worth of man,
truth,
Honesty, selflessness and nationalism
Shall be aglow with pride in every
Nigerian who desires to be a truthful Nigerian
Embracing the eternal truths.

In his last message
Yes, without much ado
More than a message indeed
But one I will ne'er forget
"Close your ranks
Oh politicians: Oh scavengers of gutter-flicked naira

I will offer you bread
My heart and soul, refuge
And the fountain of everlasting peace."

A few months before I began to couch this Memoirs, I had the opportunity to read what the president that never ruled said to the judge in 1963 before being sentenced for treasonable felony. Like a literary orator who believes both in reading and writing, the following is a few of what he said: "I must say, and this may have to be taken up with a higher tribunal, that I do not agree with your Lordship's verdict, and the premises on which it is based.

"For upwards of 30 years, I have been in politics in Nigeria; during this period I have operated in various important theaters in the life of this great Federation. I have, with others, fought against British imperialism with all my might, and with all the talents that it pleased God to give me.

"Together with other nationalists, some of whom are with me and many of whom are not with me here, we have successfully thrown out British imperialism and enthroned Africans in positions which, 20 years ago, they never dreamed of occupying."

Needless to tell you that those patriotic letters, carved into his oration shook my heart to bleed and I proceeded to think if there will ever be a true patriot, ready to rule or govern himself before governing others.

Chapter Twenty-Two

Fela Kuti Rocks the City of Vienna

In 1981, I went to Fela Kuti's performance in a Vienna Hall, located in the Third District of the city. The hall was filled to capacity. I was glad that he did come to Austria for the first time. Many times, the maestro had been to Germany but he had not set his feet on the Austrian soil until then. As always, his dancers danced like fireflies—rocking their bodies like rockers and setting on fire (without fuel) the waltzing legs of the Austrian dancers. Everyone seemed to get his/her money's worth.

After one of his intermissions, I gestured to one of his security officers to allow me to see the chief priest, as Fela was popularly called. The security officer said the chief priest was too busy to see me. Thus I wrote a note and asked the security officer to give it to him. The un-uniformed officer delivered my note accordingly. Seconds later, the maestro asked the security officer to tell me to come. A few steps before I got to his *spiritual territory*, I felt the presence of his spiritual bodyguards disarming me. My spirit was powerless, harmless.

The content of my note was very brief—thanking him for his exceptional courage to always delivering his protest songs to the doorsteps of the corrupt politicians in particular, and to the would-be corrupt political practitioners in general. I also had a paragraph on my note which honored him for being the sole international musician who had endured the highest number of detentions in the 20th century. To this, he laughed winsomely and then told me that there were a thousand corrupt politicians in each of the countries around the world but Nigeria has a thousand and one. After releasing a puff from his adroitly held cigarette, he enunciated that it was his duty to first of all remove every corrupt politician in his country (before removing others) as the political world is decaying, in trouble, ailing, and sometimes tumbling and roller-coastering.

His philosophy is simple: put the government in the hands of those who know where the shoe pinches. Hence the MOP—Movement of the People—his dream political party which he was not allowed to register. Of course, if he had contested and won any election, MOP could have been retained as the name of his party on becoming the president of Nigeria.

Fela's music might hold an international pendulum—swinging back and forth, blaring messages to the four corners of the world, howbeit it was I.K. Dairo that brought international honor to Nigeria by becoming the first African musician to be awarded MBE by the Queen of England in 1963. (It was reported that the Queen was mesmerized and unbelievably charmed by his voice and the manner he played his accordion.) In fairness to Fela Kuti, his contribution to the world music is more than MBE—Member of the British Empire, for if the Queen had invited him because of it, he could have politely rejected her invitation.

In March 1982, four months prior to the completion of my Master's program at Webster University, the loving Olodumare, the king of kings and the lord of lords brought Maria Szuts and I together as husband and wife. In July, the same year, she gave birth to Godwin Akintunde Ogunyemi.

This is the story I related to Godwin as he was growing up to become a young man. Two young boys, Kuku and Mori, grew up as friends in Lilydom. They went to school together in Lilydom. After finishing schooling, Kuku decided to become a farmer. He worked hard and within two years, he became prosperous. His parents were proud of him.

Mori did nothing but drinking with the money he received from his parents. His parents always advised him to work and do something for himself instead of asking money from them. But he did not listen to them. After three years of squandering his parent's money, his parents stopped giving him money.

A few weeks later, Mori became a beggar. As he was begging from house to house and from farm to farm, he met his friend, Kuku—surprised. He wept when Kuku told him how big and prosperous he was. Kuku told him that it was foolishness and shame not to have listened to his parents. Before he left Kuku's farm, he assured Kuku that he would change and do something for his life—making laziness and life of debaucheries history.

Either by accident or by design, four months before Godwin was born, Tina Emich, another princess in my life, gave birth to Julia Bosede Emich. It was at this juncture, I started to remember what the Indian palmist prophesied that it has pleased Olodumare, the Supreme Being to make me a centenarian on the surface of the earth and to have the fortune of meeting princesses who would fill my cup of honey to the brim. From all accounts, my luck with princesses could not be regarded as accident but as something godly, divinely and heavenly designed by Creator-Philosopher Olorun himself. Thus I have no reason to whine, pout or kvetch.

This is the story I related to Julia Bosede as she was growing up to become a young woman. In the town of Toto, there were three beautiful girls. They were always seen in eye-catching and expensive clothes bought for them by their rich boyfriends. Despite their gift of beauty, they lacked good manners, conflated with dyed-in-the-wool attitudes Because of bad manners and attitudes, their boyfriends never proposed to marry them.

Also in the same town, there were three girls who were not beautiful in the sense of facial attraction and bodily appearance. Despite the fact that they were not beautiful, they were loved by one and all due to their good characters that Toto valued above beauty and expensive apparels and jewels. Many times, they were sad because they had no boyfriends.

One fateful day during the festival of Oshun, the Divinity-Philosopher of beauty and productivity, which required every woman to wear a beautiful dress and dance before the queen, these three girls had nothing beautiful to wear. When the news reached the ears of the three rich men who were the boyfriends of the three beautiful girls, they proposed to them and married them before the festival came to a close.

Chapter Twenty-Three

Inside the Riddle of Fate

In 1983, the year my appointment with International Atomic Energy Agency ended, I set up an in-house Institute of Creative Writing in Vienna, promoting research in Nigerian/African literatures through seminars, conducted lectures, symposia, conferences, book presentations and writing workshops. Is it a riddle that I should do this in a country whose tongue is not English? If it is a riddle, it stands to reason that I will need some kind of ingenuity for elucidation.

Before I could find out why fate was treating me like this, I saw myself in the same year of 1983, as a co-founder/secretary of Austro-Nigeria Society, promoting the political, economic and cultural relationships between Austria and Nigeria. This happened when I became the elected Assistant Secretary General of the Nigerian Students' Union: a position which I reluctantly accepted due to the Muse which had forced me into the republic of letters.

Meetings of the Austro-Nigerian Society were held every month. In one of its meetings, I suggested that a Union of Nigerian Ambassadors/High Commissioners be formed so that seminal ideas as to make Nigeria one of the developed countries in the world should be, must be the concerns of those Ambassadors/High Commissioners posted to developed countries where roads, water supplies, electricity, telephones and other communications are evidences good governments, in the hands of good leaders in developed countries. The sky, in spite of its distance from the earth, is no doubt the limit if a visionary leader seriously plans to help his/her country. It is my belief that what one man can do, another man can do it, given the same environment and the same education. Apropos of development, the contra argument is that a country that always experiences bad weathers will find it very difficult to develop itself. But will there be any reason why the telephones or the electricity—for example—are not parts of the enjoyments of the citizens?

The society also subscribed to the philosophy of North-South Dialogue which Dr. Bruno Kriesky had whole-heartedly aided. But the success of the society was that there were more commercial activities between Nigeria and Austria. More Nigerians have a better knowledge of Austrian geo-politics as more Austrians do about Nigeria geo-politics. The relationship was cordial and reciprocal. And whenever and wherever a relationship is cordial and reciprocal, fears will be eliminated.

During the official inauguration of the society, His Excellency Ambassador Umar, the charismatic Nigerian chairman of the society has the following to say: "Ladies and Gentlemen, Distinguished Guests from embassies and international organizations, I am very pleased today to speak at the inauguration of the Austro-Nigerian Society. Austria and Nigeria have a long history of friendship. It started in 1974 when Austria opened its embassy in Lagos and Nigeria had its in Vienna. Since then the relationship between the two countries has always been smooth, cordial and commendable until 1967 when the diplomatic tie between the two countries was severed as Austria supported the break away Biafra during the civil war. Immediately after the war, the broken tie was re-tied again and the two nations re-established their diplomatic missions.

"Today, Austria has many industries in partnership with Nigeria. There are a number of Austrian students now carrying out their research projects in Nigerian institutions. And the number of Nigerian students, private and on scholarship, studying in Austria during the last five years has increased twofold. This is an indication that a society of this nature is good and healthy.

"My special gratitude goes to Yemi D. Ogunyemi and Robert Brunner for their cooperation that led to the creation of this society, known as the Austro-Nigerian society. It is my hope,

142

my prayer and my belief that as this society is growing from strength to strength, other countries with diplomatic ties with Austria will follow suite.

"Most people think that Nigeria should become a developed country by 2020. I agree with them, for the country suffers no shortage of manpower necessary to launch the country into the domain of miracles and excellence and when it comes to natural resources, we have enough to make an impact, inside and outside of the country, knowing full well that an impact is one of the yardsticks to determine whether a country is developing or has been developed. My immediate concern after the inaugural meeting of this society is to travel to a number of developed cities in Europe in order to see how their infrastructure are being built and how to learn from them. This is not what I can do by myself alone. Other colleagues of mine around the world will join hands with me. In developed countries, there are many *ideas at the touch of buttons* and Nigeria can learn from these ideas.

"Ladies and Gentlemen, Distinguished Guests from embassies and international organizations, the Austro-Nigerian Society is officially inaugurated. Thank you very much for supporting it morally and financially. The society will always be counting on you."

My joy was endless and my gourd of felicity was more than half full when Austrian journalists eventually ended their social war against Africa, as they no longer ridiculed Africans in some of their sensational newspapers as barbarians, even as cannibals. Sooner than later, they were enlightened about the cradle of mankind, so I thought. It took a number of protest letters to accomplish this. And I did not write less than two to the Kronen Zeitung, the sole tabloid at the heart of this inflammatory news to the innocent and often peace-loving Austrians who consumed them with gusto. Most Africans, with little or no modern education, regarded the Kronen Zeitung as the newspaper with annoying and sorrowful tales—crucifying truths, giving birth to rib-racking sensations, needed to alleviate boredom at the

Sunday breakfast tables. One aggrieved diplomat who went to the extent of having a dialogue with an Austrian officer in the Ministry of Foreign Affairs, called the reporters of the yellow journalism, working with the tabloid, natterjacks who had no respect for their ancestors. But my friends who could not hide their disappointments called the reporters chinchillas with foul pens.

Nineteen eighty-four was not that eventful. But glory will I give to God that Maria Szuts had her second son, Michael Olukayode Ogunyemi. At this point in my life, when so much was going well with my writing, I had vowed never to dream of a princess. Sooner than expected, I realized that man would do everything to propose, while God does more than everything to dispose.

Nineteen eighty-four was also the year I had a three-week work-study with the Church of Scientology in Vienna, a religion founded by L. Ron Hubbard in 1952, whose philosophy is to develop the mind, the spirit, and personal enlightenment through dianetics. I came across lots of books written by L. Ron Hubbard. And I read a few of them which are very interesting but do not show me a clear-cut path leading to spiritual enlightenment. Reading those books by L. Ron Hubbard makes me believe that becoming a writer may be interesting and supremely uplifting but won't be easy.

This is the story I handed over to Michael. In Sisal Village, it had not rained for a long time. The weather was extremely hot. Lakes and rivers were drying up. The villagers had taken to sleeping outside—under baobabs coconuts and palmettos. One such a sweltering hot day Babago and his son, Kaye were sitting under a baobab whose neighbor was a coconut. All of a sudden, Kaye shifted his position to sitting under the coconut tree. Babago quickly told him to come back and sit under the baobab, saying that the coconuts could fall at anytime and hit him on the head—with or without the assistance of the wind. Kaye did not hearken to the voice of his father. He told his father that nothing would occur.

Thirty minutes later, a robust coconut fell and hit him on the forehead. The spot where the coconut landed quickly swelled to a size of a thumb. The native medical doctor attended to him but the swelling did not shrink in size. It looked very much like a horn on a yet-to-be mature goat.

Whenever Kaye was asked why he was carrying a horn like a goat, he would not hesitate to blame himself. "The coconut fell and hit my forehead. It is my fault, my stubbornness," he would say.

Thus in 1986, as I was on the trot, interviewing Women in Europe, for the publication of a book which is eventually known as *Women In Europe*, I had a one-night stand with Elizabeth Musitz. Three months after the publication of the book, the news came to my doorstep that Elizabeth, my fourth and the last European princess, gave birth to Katharina Omoyemi Musitz. I was surprised much as I was doubtful, wondering how a one-night stand could produce a bouncing baby girl. This is not the gift of the gab—certainly. It is a gift of something in the realm of multiplying which will one day turn mortality into immortality (Is this my own contribution to the saying, "Go forth to the world and multiply?" which the citizens of the world are striving to achieve. Can we achieve this? If having children means one generation after another, it could also mean the continuity of the world. And if the world continues without being perished, would it one day please Creator-Philosopher Olodumare to turn mortality into immortality? Time will tell.

This is the story narrated to Katharina. Once upon a time, there were deposits of gold at the foot of Mount Terra. Also there were deposits of gold on its summit. Majority of the gold lovers collected their deposits of gold at the foot of the auriferous mount while a few would risk their necks and collect their deposits of gold at the summit in addition to what they had collected at the foot of the mount. Those going to the summit claimed that the deposits gold on the top were finer and bigger.

Mary and her mother Mamalove did collect their share of gold at the bottom of Mount Terra and were apparently content.

One Monday morning, as Mamalove was going to work, Mary told her she would stay away from school that day as she was not feeling well. She had lied to her mother.

No sooner Mamalove closed the door behind her than Mary dressed up and headed toward Mount Terra. On getting to the mount, she joined a column of five boys and girls, going to the top of the mount. A few meters before they reached their destination, the six of them fell, and started rolling to the foot of the mount. They sustained bruises on their legs, hands and faces by the time they got to the foot of the auriferous landmark. She was in pain like the other five.

She cried and sobbed. Her parents were surprised to realize that their good only daughter could be so greedy as to tell a lie. That year, she could not take her final exams. Although her parents took care of her, they did not stop blaming her for lying and for not obeying them.

Chapter Twenty-Four

My Contact with Africans and Africa

Post-positively, "forward ever, backward never," became the motto I always saw in my dream, shortly after I was introduced to Father Paul whose original homeland is Switzerland. After finishing his monastic training in Austria, he decided not to go back to Switzerland. His house was like a meeting place for many African students on Sundays. He was kind not only to me but also to a lot of African students from more than twenty African countries—twenty-two to be precise. Most of us paid him back by attending his church which is in the vicinity of his house.

Proud of their countries, many African students invited him to visit their countries. He accepted all their invitations and in 1971, he visited Ghana. After one year's stay in Ghana, he came back to Austria in 1972. In 1974 he visited Nigeria and having stayed in Nigeria for a few months, he left for Sierra-Leone where he carried out his missionary duties from 1974 to 1979.

On seeing what he had done for mankind by helping everyone he knew—showing love and compassion, I encouraged him to write his autobiography entitled *My Contact With Africans and Africa.*

In 1989, the book was published by Development News, Ltd which I had set up in Vienna in 1983, with a branch in Lagos.

Life was sympathetic with Father Paul and as some reports had it, he behaved badly like most celibates. Father Paul did everything to convince his congregation in Vienna that he was a human being who, for all indications, and for all evidences, tried to live as a man who was called by the Holy Ghost to carry the Cross of Salvation. It seemed he found no Cross of Salvation in Europe. Thus he had his eyes on the innocent continent of Africa.

Whether that was why he had been planning to spend the rest of his life in Africa was not clear. What was clear is that he left for Kenya in 1991, telling one and all that Africa is his home. Two years later, he paid his debt to nature. I lost a friend whose kindness I could not requite before he drank the cup of mortality. But I still have a copy of his book which I cherish very much—no less than an object from a holy place or a memento from Aladdin's Cave or the grove of Olumo Rock

Chapter Twenty-Five

Women in Europe

What pushed me to write *Women In Europe* in 1986 was unclear. Was it a Holy Spirit who had regaled on something shared with Divinity-Philosopher Ogun, the Commander-in-Chief of metals? Or could it be the spirits of the ancestors, spear-headed by the spirit of my father? And one should not forget that it could be in the creature of Ijapa, the folk hero and the fabled protagonist of antiquity in Yoruba folktales. All I know is that the spirit did not come from the realm of a European Muse. The Muse was unequivocally African. No one wants to deny this, for 1986 was the very year Africans in Africa and Africans in Diaspora saw an African (in the person of Wole Soyinka) being awarded a Nobel Prize in Literature.

The unfathomable spirit gently nudged me to interview all the European women in the summer of 1986. First I was reluctant, fearing that I could stumble and fall. And to my way of thinking, stumbling and falling, douses the spirit of immortality which I have been able to woo and keep—watching it jealously—with the courtesy of Olodumare. But the same unfathomable good spirit asked me to act like a man—fearing no one except the Supreme Being and his established authorities.

Between 1986 and 1993, the book had circulated to a number of families in Austria. Some of the women's and even men's reactions were ugly much as they were embarrassing. Some scowled at me. Some pouted. Some twisted their eyebrows. While some twisted their noses toward the vault of heaven, some winked successively as though beams or grains of paradise had penetrated into their eyes. The reason why I was attacked by these facial expressions is that a portion, just a portion of my book had flayed the conservative dignity of the

Austrian families by daring to let them know that by sparing the rod, they would spoil the child.

I defended the book before those who had interviewed me by saying that such a book, promoting women studies, is overdue. A book about women in Europe, written by an African, married to one of the daughters of the land, is overdue. This is the line taken by my wife and my in-laws.

As a stubborn qualm was molesting me months later, I felt like expurgating that which had caused some sleepless nights to some families. But an American writer, Richie, who I met in the American library said I had uprooted no flower that stopped the bees from obtaining their nectar, adding that I am protected by freedom of speech to express myself as long as what I am expressing is not obnoxious or something that would lead to debaucheries.

Said Richie, "If you are dreaming of becoming a serious writer, you had better leave for an English-speaking country."

"What country will you recommend?"

"I will recommend the United States."

"Why the United Sates?"

"I am recommending the United States not because it is my country but because it is a land of dreams. If you know how to dream and how to fashion your dreams into new ideas, the United States will be your promised land."

"A promised land?"

"Yes a promised land. A land where you can turn your dreams into ideas and your ideas into action, is a promised land—flowing with milk and honey."

"You mean all will be well with me should I pack and go to America?"

"Absolutely. Your books will be published and you will be on the top of your game. Additionally, you will become a beneficiary of the Civil Rights Movement, like."

"You mean my work will not be considered as coming from a distant land?"

"Even if your work originates from the distant land, the bottom line is that it will be published and you will be considered a veritable member of the intellectual elite."

"I am so happy to hear this good news, Richie. It makes me feel as though I am born today. It gladdens my heart of hearts to know that Rodney King's incident of 1991 was a mistake, an act of God in all probability and palpability."

The American writer helped uplift my spirits, for my futuristic caveat is that any mistake, light or egregious, made in Europe or America would be repeated in Africa, since we tend to consume almost everything from Europe and America.

Days later I came to realize why some people were upset as a result of my good- intentioned criticism. They were upset because I am an invisible writer, writing in a visible environment. I can only be visible if and when I carried a gun, owned a gun or do something outrageous. But while thinking of Ralph Ellison, I said to myself that I am a creature of substance from my family's point of humility. I am a creature of blood, flesh and bones—with adequate liquid regards in my veins, waiting for the Almighty Father to bear me from the Pearly Gates to his abode of his perpetual bliss when I pass on.

Educationally, and with culture sharing a consequential part of what education stands for, both of which are consumed as one travels, my going to Europe is to consume something that I could pass on to my children—tomorrow—to consume without

151

stomachache or borborygmus. Looking back and examining the past and the present, I find out that it is the first time I would see Europeans fretting over a triviality in contrast to mammoth of misnomers which Africans had embraced with smiles and miles. How I wished I could give copies of the book to the children for whom the rod had not been spared.

But there is still a bag hanging in the air, swinging back and forth. It is a bag whose contents are unknown. As long as its contents are unknown, I will not know why the Supreme Being had made me a creature of a man whose gourd is invariably filled with honey by princesses. Am I not getting myself into trouble— buying trouble which I cannot pay for, for being an accessory to those who have regarded themselves as *woman killers*?

Chapter Twenty-Six

The Grains of Paradise

In 1987, I had the blessing to visit Nigeria. I was very delighted much as I was curious after many years of self-exile that resulted into voluntary slavery. The Aeroflot, being the cheapest flight in Vienna, Austria was my choice. With a night stop-over in Moscow, and a one-hour stop-over in Tripoli, Libya, the carrier then landed at the Murtala Mohammed International Airport in Lagos. Apostle Adewale Ogunyemi, my younger brother, who has joined the rank and file of the landlords in Lagos, was already waiting for me at the airport. I was more than happy to see him, a likable workaholic in the family. Hugging him after so many years of punishing myself in the midst of happiness, hope and self-sufficiency is like hugging a khalasi who worked very hard to become a master. I was very enthusiastic to see other members of my family too. I was joyous to hear that those who were dead are living and those who are living are being resuscitated. I had a mental visit to my father's rest-in-the-Lord place. But a physical one, I could have lovingly preferred if not because time was against me—brutally tormenting me.

I could see that many things had changed for the better. Bridges, more bridges have been built in many parts of Lagos. Of these bridges, the most spectacular one is the Third Mainland Bridge that stretches from the Island to the mainland of Ebute Metta, over the lagoon. And the second one is the Lagos-Epe bridge (via Lekki), making the distance betwixt Lagos and Epe three times shorter than before. Even roads are planned to reach all the littoral town-lets and villages. Life has come back to where life belongs.

The changeling carrying the news of the super highway technology has already visited the land. Sometimes, it would crow like a rooster. Sometimes it would roar like the king of the beasts. Whether crowing or roaring, the people have got the news of its preparedness. Thus the roads are bigger, reaching the farmers' supply lines. There are shelters at the bus stops. The water is running day and night. The electricity, reaching many villages—is turning nights into days. The canoe-owners were paddling. The boaters were rowing. The garbage collectors are dutifully collecting the trash. The peddlers, about a million, have revamped the economics of peddling. Indigenous restaurants (bukarias), are busy like bees and booming like the business of the central market. The public telephones, once said to be a luxury have turned every corner of the street into a chatterbox. Tourism, once said to be unnecessary has turned the cities into international tourist destinations—with the faces of the so-called black, white, yellow, brown tourists from all walks of life. The robbers have found honorable jobs to do. The beggars have are gainfully employed. The financial district (and the Lagos Stock Exchange) is as busy as London financial district. The pace is high. Life is livable with oil money, so it is: so it must be. Banks and hotels dot every corner of a major boulevard. The slogan is: "If you don't go, let me pass, for time is naira." I was impressed even if my eyes were closed in my head: an invisible cub of a man. But for the presence of the army outside their honorable barracks, all could have been perfect. As a matter of fact, *ne plus ultra* was the talk of the town.

The main reason why I visited my birthplace is to let my friends and acquaintances realize that I am no longer a self-exile and that I have stopped calling myself a voluntary slave. I am a man, married to a white princess whose father is a vicar and her mother, a church pianist.

The second reason which is more crucial than the first one was my search for the grains of paradise. The grains of paradise, the kola nuts and the bitter nuts are indispensable in a traditional Yoruba home. The grains of paradise, the first kind of spice known to mankind, is used to cure many things. It can be chewed—regaling on it for the sake of its aroma. It can be used with the word of amen. It can be used with certain ointment and applied to cicatrices, especially if a child is thought to be, or behaving like abiku—a child, tormenting its parents by being born many times and dying as many times as it pleases.

So I succeeded in finding some with the help of Apostle Ade Ogunyemi, my younger brother. And I brought them to Vienna to apply ritualistically to my second son, Godwin Akintunde, who was thought to be behaving like an abiku child. (He had fainting feats.)

Months later, my princess confessed that the child must have suffered concussion as he fell off the table when he was a few months old. This is why he had fainting feats. He is no abiku child. For my spouse not to tell me on time (just because she was scared of the consequences as she later related) drew a nail of annoyance into my skull. Olodumare in his omnipresence and benevolence quickly removed my annoyance and substituted it with a spirit of forgiveness, an integral part of his unconditional love. I own him many words of gratitude. Love can be made perfect if one works on it with the help of God. To be a father is to become a MAN. Otherwise the children will find it difficult to find the light at the end of the tunnel. As per an African adage, it takes a village to raise a child to become a MAN. Not many children have such an opportunity. Many did not make it because there was no MAN or WOMAN at the time they were growing up. For example, not many grown-ups (let alone children) look back and find the cause of their missteps whenever they stumble and fall.

Chapter Twenty-Seven

How Dogs Become Friends of Men

Published in 1987, *How Dogs Become Friends of Men* is one of the few books I took with me when I visited Nigeria in 1987. A dog is Ogun's favorite animal in Atlantic Yoruba. Every dog knows this. Whenever a dog is tied to a post, it will quickly develop the instinct conflated with dread that it is going to be sacrificed to Ogun, the commander-in-chief of iron and steal.

The reason why I wrote the book is twofold. The first one simply tells the story of how dogs, came from the wild to become the human beings' best friends.

The second reason is fuller. And this is how it began. In 1974, the year I first landed in Vienna, I met a sixty-five-year old man at Schottenring, a few minutes of padding to the financial/commercial part of Vienna. He was walking his brown-haired collie. The dog must have got the instinct that I am from a family where dogs are butchered for the family god, for it came to me and started to brush my trousers with its tail— apparently appealing to me to spare its life. I was delighted, thinking that the man and his pet must be friendly creatures by nature. I reciprocated by trying to pat the pet on the head.

All of a sudden, the pet's owner asked, "Young man, where are you from?"

"I am from the continent of Africa, the cradle of mankind according to my history teacher."

"What country in Africa?" he rejoined with a dignified air of knowing Africa pretty well and then on removing his pipe from his mouth, spat decently, gentlemanly. The spitting sound was almost inaudible like the defecating sound of an overhead subway pigeon.

"The most populous country in Africa," I rejoined, brushing my goatee.

"Yes I know, Nigeria. My histo-geography is not fooling me."

"You are as correct as correctness."

"Let me ask you this, and do not be offended," he said in a near-yodeling voice. "Are some of the Africans still living on tree-tops?"

My shanks shook for irritation. My head ached for disappointment. My mouth pouted for indignation. I shuddered as though I was going to fetch a punch from my pocket as one of my hands was groping for a nondescript. But I managed sooner than expected to put myself under control. Consequently, I said to this masasaur of a man, "My friend, Africa is no stranger to miracles, myths and phenomena. Things happen there everyday, keeping in shape peoples of different hues—black, white, yellow, brown and even red. But I am happy to let you know that I know a family that lives on a tree-top and your ambassadorial residence which is also on a tree-top is a few feet away. Each day, there are greetings of friendliness and good will such as Good-morning, Good-afternoon, Good-evening, Good-night, ambassador."

"Das gibts doch nicht,"—meaning *that's impossible or I don't believe it,* he enunciated. He was surprised. He did not expect an affirmative reply, attaching his own accredited ambassador to the derision or pleasantry he wanted to dump over the innocence of the African people.

"Why not? It is possible. Is it not our custom to sleep on trees? I guess I am not barking up the wrong tree. Will it not be polite for your accredited ambassador to respect and behave

158

according to the culture of the land, knowing full well that when you are in Rome, you do as Romans?"

He looked somehow defeated. As a matter of fact, he was a defeated man. Then he yielded his lips to a munificent smile which graduated into a genuine grin on seeing that I reciprocated without a temperamental chagrin. Holding me by hand, he prayed me to follow him to a nearby coffee house for a cup of coffee. I followed him like a student following a professor of novel ideas.

On taking our seats in Rita's Coffee House, one of Vienna's elegant and popular coffee houses, he asked the waitress to bring two coffees. But I interjected and requested the jaunty waitress that my choice should be a cup of cappuccino.

Harrumphing and opening his mouth like a professor who had found a solution to a puzzle, for which he had been cudgeling his brains for days band nights, he introduced himself as Heinz Baumeister, a journalist who had just started his retirement having worked for twenty-five years with the *Presse,* the most popular newspaper in Austria. He gave me his business card which showed him as Herr Dr. Heinz Baumeister, editor of *Die Presse.*

I introduced myself as Johnny-come-lately who had just begun to learn German so that I could study Mass Communication.

A few seconds after my introduction, he said, "Young man, it is not my intention to offend you and your culture but I am a humorist and a joker. I make jokes everyday. I derive a kind of satisfaction making humors. Jokes have become the weft and warp of my being. Even my wife sometimes pinches me when I make an expensive joke."

"Jokes and humors are part of life. They both bring jollity and joie de vivre."

"My friend, I know they are part of life but sometimes when I am carried away I make an expensive one."

"Then you have to pay for it."

"Now I am paying for what I had jocularly said to you." He laughed and forced me to do likewise.

"How long will you continue to make expensive jokes if you don't check yourself?"

"My friend, my head is too funny. And my jokes had cost me something."

"Cost you something?"

"Yes. About a year ago, I made a joke, in the presence of my daughter and my wife that Africans were/are cannibals. Three months later, my daughter had an African boyfriend. One day while breakfasting, my daughter said to me and her mother that she would never come back to live with us." He paused with a wry.

"Why?"

"Because I said Africans are cannibals. What she said to me in her words is, 'My boyfriend is a human being like you. He treats me better than my former Austrian boyfriend. He is no cannibal. *Nein*, he has no history of cannibalism. So you can live here with your dream of cannibalism and your funny and hurtful tales. But should you need a pithecanthropus, buy your round ticket and go to the back of beyond—as far away as Bullamakanka.'"

"How old is she?"

"She is just twenty-one and about to finish her Master Degree in family law."

"So you have lost something more important than something?" He shook his head and I thought I saw a wink of regret in his ocean-blue eyes. This time he seemed not to know either how to find the loss or how to pay for the loss. This is a human loss. He is the only one who can find...Alas!

I did not see the sixty-five years old Heinz after our first meeting. But we did phone each other until the line of communication fainted and then became stone-dead.

In 1987, as fate would have it, I ran into Heinz while swanning around during the fifth month of the year and enjoying the scent and fragrance of the morning-glories. He was happy to see me, as I was happy to see him. This time his collie did not accompany him. A lousy joke inside me was that he must have lost a man's best friend as he had lost his only daughter. Also, I noticed that his beard was more prominent than his chin. Because our accidental meeting place was close to where we first met, we decided to patronize the same popular and elegant coffee. The inside of the coffee house was more or less the same as it was thirteen years ago except that the cheerful waitress had left for another job.

No sooner we began to sip modicums from our cups than he pulled out *How Dog Become Friends of Men* from his media bag. I was astonished much as I was delighted to see that he had a copy of a book published barely four months ago.

"This is your book, young man. You're an author in Austria, a non-English-speaking country."

I thanked him for recognizing a small piece of labor and told him that it is my hope that Creator-Philosopher Olodumare would make me do better.

"What is Olodumare?" He asked in a voice characteristic of a rush-hour tourist.

"Olodumare is God in Yoruba."

"Yoruba people, I heard of their king in Lagos. I read also of Ile-Ife where they are originated. They occupy the Western part of Nigeria. They are famous for their terra-cotta works."

"Thank you, Heinz. Your knowledge about the Yoruba people is remarkable. I am impressed. You should throw your heart in the ring and visit Nigeria before you second retirement." He laughed and I was scared that he was going to make another annoying but good-humored sentence in the name of a brain-teaser.

"I have been brainstorming since last year when your countryman won the Nobel Prize in literature."

"Oh Wole Soyinka."

"Yes that is his name. Did he grow up as infant prodigy like Wolfgang Amadeus Mozart?"

"This, I can't tell. Some people say he is a miracle child who started to show his intellect at the age of two and a half."

"How does he become a house-power of good English which is as good as anyone in all Commonwealth countries?"

"I think by working very hard, day and night."

"Would he one day produce the first Nigerian English Dictionary?"

"That is possible. Some even think he should be the editor-in-chief of the Concise Oxford English Dictionary and the once proposed but abandoned Commonwealth English Dictionary. But time is always a big factor for a serious writer."

"He must be an infant prodigy. However, I have difficulty in pronouncing his name."

"It's not so difficult. Just try to pronounce it everyday, you will master it. Has he put Nigeria on the world map?"

"Absolutely. He is not only a poet of substance. He is equally a first class dramatist."

"There is another good writer too."

"Chinua Achebe?"

"Yes, he is a good novelist: author of *Things Fall Apart,* the first African bestseller."

"Have you tried to ski since you came?"

"No. Skiing will be the last thing I will do while breathing my last."

"You know this is number one winter sport in Austria and indeed in all Europe?"

"I know. I know it is thrilling when the skiers are running or ski jumping. But for my money, I prefer to watch them over the television."

"By the way, have you been to the residence of the Habsburg Family?"

"You mean the Schoenbrunn?"

"Yes, the Empress Maria Theresa's palace."

"I was there several times."

"How did you find it?"

"I found it very quaint and impressive. The well-pruned hedges surrounding the footpaths, the pretty gardens and Gloriettes added an extra décor and luster to the palace. Some of its rooms will be ideal as a writer's retreat."

"What about the zoo?"

"I was there also."

"Built in 1752, it is the world oldest zoo."

"So I was told."

"As you must have been told, Habsburgs were a family that ruled Austria for over 700 years, marrying within the family. They were not a fighting family per se, for they regaled on exquisite arts and aesthetics of their time."

"Is it true that Empress Maria Theresa actually gave birth to sixteen children?"

"It is true. Records have showed that none of her sixteen children died at infancy."

"Sixteen children? It sounds to me like a cock and bull story from a land of fairies. She must have been the most fertile empress in her days."

"I don't think any other empress in the world beats her to the first place in her days. Maybe in Africa?" He laughed between an impending use of metaphors and ironies, and the smoky air oozing from his mouth filled the breeze above my nostrils with the smell of the Cuba-made cigars. The cigars nearly made me queasy. Because he is a gentleman who did not complain about how his smoking was polluting the atmosphere of the coffee house, I did not also complain about how his smoking was twisting out of shape my nose. I rubbed my nose repeatedly but I did not complain. According to my father, the worth of man is known in the moment of an adversity. Not that I did not like cigars which I used to smoke between 1990 and 1991 when I belonged to the class of the movers and shakers of the Vienna Social Circle, but this is 1987. Yemi is a married gentleman now, and has children. I must keep my non-smoking vow to my spouse and to my children.

We sipped from our cups and, the friendship, first established in 1974, seemed to be metamorphosing into a new dimension of camaraderie.

Chortling and placing his hand on mine, which was on the table, as though he wanted both of us to enter into a universal cult, he said in a voice that fell to a whisper, "Herr Dr; I want to tell you why men and women are friends of dogs: why the world loves dogs like a faithful servant. Long, long time ago, (before Christianity or any other modern religion), there was a dog which was very faithful to its master. The dog was so helpful to its owner, so much that its owner regarded it as its chum. At the time the man was dying, he said the D-O-G was his G-O-D, a supernatural helper. Thus D-O-G became G-O-D in English."

"What are you driving at?"

"What I am driving at is that the supernatural spirit we call God in English, and Olodumare or Olorun in Yoruba, respectively, tells no human being his name. We human beings give him names. We name him. Whatever we call him passes from one generation to another as does an oral literature."

"This is very interesting to know. This will be the greatest *scratch of knowledge* in my life."

"And this is why your book, **How Dogs Become Friends of Men** is a thoughtful and wonderful book, howbeit its smallness."

I stumbled into reflection while my friend regaled on his pipe. The atmosphere was a relaxed one as more and more people came to wash their throats with coffee and enliven the evening with political news and social accounts. Added to the congenial atmosphere was Wolfgang Amadeus Mozart's dulcet roundelay that nearly induced me to improvise a nocturne.

On asking him the whereabouts of his friend, collie, he told me that he unfortunately met his death in 1986 while crossing the street and hit by a car. He could not sue the motorist because it was his fault for allowing the man's best friend to get loose of his line. I comforted him by saying that although he had lost a good friend, he had not lost his jokes, the kernels of his happiness.

After the second cup of coffee for him and a second cup of cappuccino for me, we departed, longing for another meeting as soon as the time in the bosom of Creator-Philosopher Olorun permitted it.

Chapter Twenty-Eight

Going Against the Grain

Our third meeting came up on July 5, 1987, the first anniversary of my lastborn, Katharina Omoyemi Musitz. This time, we decided to meet at Coffee Aida. Coffee Aida is not as popular and elegant as Rita Coffee but it affords one the opportunity to sit upstairs and be able to watch almost everything happening on Karntner Street, the most popular and the sole place where one could feel the pulse of the city of Vienna. In view was the Gothic Stephansdom, (St. Stephen's Cathedral) a magnificent landmark-church, said to have been built in 1511. Earlier, in the day, I went to the British Bookshop at 24, Weihburggasse Street, off Karntner Street and delivered three titles of my books—*Women in Europe, African Soul* and *How Dogs Become Friends of Men.*

No sooner we sat down and started washing our throats with cappuccino and coffee, respectively, than he asked me if I am married. I told him I am married and blessed with five God-given pretty children.

"Is the lucky one from your country?"

"No, she is from your country."

"This is good for you as a writer."

"Why is that?"

"Because she will help you understand the political, the economic and the cultural history of Austria as you develop your writing."

"What an advantage! Should there be anyone, I should seize it with gratitude, for I will recognize the fact that my success in writing cannot be healthy without her help."

"That is exactly what I mean. If I may ask, is polygamy still practiced in your country?"

"Yes it is still being practiced. I think it will continue to be practiced the end of time?"

"Does it worry you?"

"Not a bit. Why it does not worry me is that research has shown that every man in every society seems to be a polygamist. Here in Austria, a married man who has a girlfriend seems to be practicing polygamy. Researches have also shown that no one part of the world has ever existed without polygamy. Polygamy lives because there are men to show women their masculine love and there are women to reciprocate femininely."

"Who is Oduduwa?" he asked as though to test my knowledge on the anthropological evolution of the Yoruba people.

"Oduduwa is the primogenitor, the king and the founder of the Yoruba people and their folk philosophy. Because he was a king, every daughter and every son in Yorubaland can be called a princess or a prince, respectively."

"Are you a prince, Herr Doctor?"

"Thou sayeth." And a crooked but winsome smile caressed the contour of my countenance.

"Have you any political ambition."

"No. Politics is no longer my cup of lemon tea. It is too dirty for me to dabble in. I don't want to plunge into a privileged whirlwind or whirligig. I will rather work hardest so as to enjoy a green and fruitful retirement like you. For if the writers always ask for the Muse's guidance, they will invariably be regarded as soothsayers or as prophets or prophetesses."

"I agree with you, taking into consideration what happened in 1986 when the charismatic and smart newspaper journalist, Dele Giwa was killed by a mail bomb."

"Is it not dirty, senseless and preposterous if a cub should die in the hands of a lioness who is supposed to protect her cub?"

"It is. As I read about Yoruba culture, I discover that every elderly man seems to be a healer?"

"This is true, for every elderly man must learn how to take care of his family. He must also learn how to take care of the health of the family. This is why my story contains the power to heal. Ifa Divination, the metaphysical concept, central to Yoruba philosophy, religion and literature is the guiding force for the Yoruba living in the continents of Africa, Americas and Europe."

He looked through the window, ogling the psychedelic throngs of beauties on the street. I also did the same, recognizing a passerby as one of my students, and my eyes fell almost simultaneously upon a player of hurdy-gurdy—turning his territory into a joyful hurly-burly. All of a sudden, I went into an artificial demise. Before this could lead me into a spiritual demise, I asked my friend why the so-called civilized whites find it Godly to always disparage Africans.

His answer was not surprising: "The white people want to stay on the top of their game. They have discovered so many modern things and they want to jealously guide them by playing the superiority card. This is a race or a battle for superiority, Herr Doctor."

"Do whites consider this kind of disparage as fair?"

"It may not be fair but the white people do not want to lose the fact that every new discovery is an evidence of supremacy."

"What must the Africans do to counteract the tomes of disparage? Must they hit back?"

"Even if they hit back, they cannot win the battle?"

"Why not?"

"Because you do not control the media. The media is the modern searing weapon which the white people are using to their utmost advantage. Until the Africans have the chance to control the world media, there is no way for them to win the battle for superiority."

While thanking me for the role played in setting up the Austro-Nigerian society, I regarded his physiognomy and said, "Heinz, you are looking good at sixty-five."

His reply was heard by a couple sitting at the table next to us, "Because I am not a polygamist but a monogamist?"

Minutes later, he called for a Wiener Schnitzel with vegetables and smashed potatoes. He wanted to order the same menu for me but I decided to order a plate of fried boneless fish with rice and vegetables. After this, we both ordered a bowl each of zakuski, a Russian hors d'oeuvres, consisting of tiny open sandwiches, spread with caviar. We both joked and luxuriated in the exchange of pleasantries of a good time that we were sharing together.

"When a people ride on the wheel of advancement
And advancement begets perpetual fear
Share it with the world."

"When a people is innocent and hospitable
Dying of innocence and hospitality
Share it with the Africans."

I told him the first lyric is for the people of my second home, Austria, while the second lyric is for the people of my first home, Nigeria. He thanked me and uttered a joke with a yodeling voice.

As the clock was chiming a count of ten, I stood up. He also stood up. Both of us were ready to go. From the Aida Coffee House, we went for a stroll along the Karntner Street to the Opera House. While shaking his hand for a good evening time with a good friend, I prayed him to write a letter of apology to his only begotten daughter. His reply was in affirmative. To write such a letter is one thing. To be accepted is another thing. But the ball is in his court, as a learned man, an elder for that matter.

Chapter Twenty-Nine

Commonwealth Literature and Language Study

Nineteen hundred and eighty-eight: As the summer was setting in, I attended the 11th Annual Conference on Commonwealth Literature and Language Studies in Aachen, Germany from 16-19 June, 1988.

On seeing the program that was spread over four days, and the list of would-be speakers, I was interested as my spirit had been yearning for something special: something challenging, creative and with international flavor. Sooner than expected, I contacted one of the organizers, asking her if I could present a paper on Nigerian literature and she agreed. She told me that Nigerian literature has been a focus since Wole Soyinka became the first African to be awarded Nobel Prize in literature in 1986.

A few hours after I had disclosed the news to my second-half, I thought of flying so that I could get there in two hours. But after a second thought, I resolved to go by train. Preparing like a soldier that I would never could be, I boarded the German-bound train on the 15th of June, about two hours after the dusk. From Vienna, Melk and Linz, I felt the cool breeze from the Danube River, the longest river in European Union and the second longest in Europe after Volga. Two hours later, the train entered Munich Railway Station. This breeze which I described at that time as Oshun's zephyr was also caressing my nostrils as the train screeched along the river towns of Passau, Regensburg and Nuremburg—all in Germany. By the time it reached Nuremburg, the eyes could already identify the position of the nose from the nostrils.

At Nuremberg Railway Station, a young lady, pulling thirty entered the train. Her hair was braided and she was carrying a rucksack. In her hand, clutched by her hennaed fingers was a copy of *ROOTS* by Alex Haley. Sitting down gingerly, almost opposite me on the left row, she started to read her book. Also in my hand at the time she boarded the train was a copy of *ROOTS*, a book relating the saga of an American family. On discovering that we were both reading the same saga of an American family, I started to look at her direction, hoping that her eyes would meet with mine. Her head was buried inside her book and I thought she was reading the book not for pleasure but for exams. On her front seat was a Turkish-looking man, reading sura. But suddenly, when least expected, when all hopes seemed to have been lost, her head went up as she was searching for a yawn and a stretch and her eyes met with mine.

Consequently, she exclaimed, "Doctor Ogunyemi, good morning."

"Good morning. But tell me, when did I receive that professorial title?"

"You don't have to receive it, you are entitled to it—with over fifteen titles—you are qualified before any institution makes you qualified."

"To receive it, is to be entitled to it. Otherwise the academia will find me doing the wrong thing."

"Professor, no academia will find you doing the wrong thing so long as you are productive the way you are."

I stopped dialoguing with a stranger but I soon realize that she is not a stranger when she opened my eyes to the past and declared her identity as Rebecca.

"This is Rebecca," I guess you still remember me.

"Rebecca George. Of course I still remember you." I said this with an air of confidence in order to replace the weakness of forgetfulness with the power of remembrance.

I could not easily recognize her as a student—my student at the Institute of Creative Writing because of her glasses which she never wore for those two weeks she participated in learning Nigerian/African literatures. She is from Bandar Seri Begawan but she lives in Britain. When she left the Institute, she told me she was going to Britain, not knowing we would sooner or later be reading the same book, inside the same train and attending the same Conference on Commonwealth Literature and Language. What a small world of coincidence!

She is a mealy-mouthed girl who is garrulous in the midst of silence.

Our conversation became lively, injecting common sense and creative passion into modernism and postmodernism, wondering why modernism did not pay attention to African literatures: why African literatures seemed to have been neglected by those who seemed to know better. Whether postmodernism or post-independence literature is more enlightening than modernism, both of us believe that African literatures have come to play a significant role in post-independence literatures. According to my knowledge, I said modernism came after the First World War to replace what a few saw as too rigid and conservative. But in the 1960s, post-modernism came to replace what a few saw as not *modern* enough.

Certainly, post-modernist ideas in the art works have influenced philosophy and the society. It has expanded the importance of critical theory and has been a point of departure and springboard for works of literature, architecture and design. It has been visible in marketing and the interpretation of history and law, as evidenced in this century.

She said there might be some people in the future who would arguably discourse that there should be civilization and post-civilization, as the 20th century is yielding to 21st century.

Referring to *ROOTS* as an indispensable book of enlightenment for anyone interested in Slave history, we both said that Alex Haley has produced an important work that must endure as long as Slave history endures. Whether the tome of a book is seen as both fiction or nonfiction, it has nevertheless generated interest in the study of African and African-American Literatures.

Lastly, I asked Rebecca to play a mock scenario of being my sister, kidnapped into slavery in 1766, chained inside a ship, reaching America in 1767. After this separation, brother and sister never met until both of them are as old and frail as skeletons. With that mock scenario, we could visualize what mental and physical pain Kunta Kinte must have undergone and endured. Although Brunei did not experience the pangs and brutality of slavery, except that she was colonized by the British from 1888 to 1984, yet Rebecca was able to dramatize the role of one bludgeoned by evocative emotions.

Slowly but steadily, the vehicular iron monster snaked all along until it was pulled to a stop at Aachen Railway Station, with an ear-pleasing screech that sent the pecking homing pigeons into four echelons. Here a friend of Rebecca was waiting for her. Here we separated at a forked street. Here she took the left street, while I took the right, hoping to meet again during the conference.

Soon after we separated, I had some strange feelings as though the station is still under the chapter and verse of the deities, as I once experienced when I first got to know the holy city of Ile-Ife, the spiritual and cultural capital of Yoruba land. Why that should be my experience, I don't know. Maybe because I had lately read German medieval book of mythology in which Mephistopheles or Mephisto is said to have purchased Faust's soul in German legend.

Not far away from the railway station was the hostel where I spent my first night with a number of Australian, English, German writers and students of Commonwealth Literatures. Each one of us had something to say about his or her career and experience with Commonwealth Literatures. At the end of the day, it looked as though we had produced a tetralogy for the conference. There were analects as well as pastiches which many of us referred to, adding sparks to our discourses. One of my questions put to my Commonwealth literature colleagues is: "When did *bildungsroman* infiltrate into English usage. No one satisfied me with an answer. However, I know *bildungsroman* (a German word) means a novel about a person's formative years. Without being disoriented in a forked road, one can easily perorate that *bildungsroman* is the same as formation or education novel.

Seeing that I found myself as the only one participant from Nigeria, I was not feeling comfortable in that I was probably the only one (who is learning to become a writer) who left behind his spouse and his four years old son. The compunction that started to trouble me is whether my leaving behind my family was worth my attending this all-important international conference. There is no easy way to defend myself because as a family matter is important, so also a professional matter. There is no gainsaying the obvious that many schools of thought, (from the Elders in particular), will infer that family responsibilities should be treated as number one, while professional responsibilities should be treated as number two.

The following morning, our first assembly took place in a hall where Lewis Nkosi, a South African writer, was one of the key speakers. After the assembly, I met Taban Lo Niyong, a Sudanese poet who proudly showed me that he could speak some Yoruba by asking me in Yoruba to translate an English word into Yoruba, which I did to his satisfaction. He also said jocularly whether my Yoruba was any longer as strong as English. I confessed to him that the vernacular languages are dying on the lips of many African English writers. He agreed with me.

As I stole cautiously into one of the conference rooms, I felt as though I was in the 16th century Germany when Gotterdammerung, the German myth was rumored to be the talk of the town. And I carried this feeling of German and Yoruba thought of mythology with me as I boarded my train the third day, heading toward Vienna. My family was more than happy to see me back in three days instead of seven days I had originally told them I would be back. The conference was a success but I had not stayed long enough to be part of that success. My mea-culpa.

Before the end of 1988, *The Yellow House* was produced, published by Development News Ltd. This is a book of short stories: my first book of short stories. Under its covers are The Stranded Tramp, How Tortoise Survived the Famine in Ogba, Surulere—Patience is a Virtue and *The Yellow House*. Two hundred and fifty copies were published. All the copies were sold out after three months. For an invisible writer in a non-English-speaking country, this I consider a bestseller.

A year after the conference on Commonwealth Literature and Language Study, is a year every literary mind must not forget, for it was a year when the life of a wordsmith was in danger. On the14[th] of February 1989, it was announced by one of the most revered beings in the Muslim World. On the Iranian Radio, Ayatollah Khomeini said the following: "I inform the proud Muslim people of the world that the author of the Satanic Verses book, which is against Islam, the Prophet and the Qur'an, and all those involved in its publication who are aware of its content are sentenced to death."

As the translation was made open to me, my eyes gathered water, my shanks shook, my scrotum shrank to a size never, witnessed before. Consequently, I began to pule like a Pastor for what I could not control like an Imam. Genuflecting beside my table, I beseeched God to always be my director in whatever I wanted to write. This is my prayer, "May I write everything: all things that will cause young and old, black and white, yellow and brown to always ask for my book in tens and twenties."

Adieu Maroko—1989: Good news again on visiting Nigeria in 1989. Life is more idyllic, compared to what I experienced in 1987. Evidently, the general outlook as it was in 1987, has moved from the glue and show to the glitz and glamour for one and all. Life has become palpably bearable despite the fact that the government has been trudging shamelessly against the grain. I noticed both physically and mentally that a floodgate has been opened to churches, mosques, schools, universities, and gambling in lieu of drug trafficking. There are phenomena of good things—peace, love, tolerance, understanding, hope, faith and creative writing. Creative Writing classes are found and held at the beaches, backyards and under the trees such as the baobabs and breadfruits. The click-clacks, click-clacks of the typewriters, albeit deafening, unequivocally add to the all-consuming feeling that the proliferation of urban pulp fiction has come to stay—permanently. Here and there are peddlers of nondescript titles padding from one street to another—in droves—and often cause traffic jams, a common phenomenon in mega cities. The slogan, "reading is good, writing is creative" resonates like tintinnabulation in my ears and I deeply felt in love with it. All this is happening because people are beginning to jump from an oral to a written literature. And they are doing this in a large number due to the fact that literacy has moved up to ninety percent in urban areas. The only thing which was apparent and sorely missing is payola which is the residue of bribery and corruption. Whatever might be the twist and turn of the metaphors and how they are employed, it is vivid to the voice coming to the ears and illuminating to the sight coming to the eyes that the army (with its finger placed on the Holy Book), is proving something: something upon which the civilian government (which is about to be born) will improve upon—with its finger and a cross laid upon the Holy Scripture. Gosh, gee, I saw and dreamt of many phenomena as perfect as a palindrome—consciously and subconsciously. There are many contrasts. Like a tourist, my vision was programmed to behold the good ones as presented.

In a trance such as this (akin to Martin Luther King's dream-prophecy), there was a concourse of black, white, brown, yellow and wheat-colored people carrying their loads of self-affliction upon their heads, moving from bathos to sublime, climbing the ladder of authority, settling in gilded cages of authority and luxuriousness such as Apapa, Ikeja, Ikoyi, Marina, Maryland, Race Course, Surulere, Victoria Island and Yaba. In order to increase the number of the gilded areas, much of the Atlantic has been reclaimed and new estate houses built. *Ne plus ultra* nearly becomes the talk of the town and could become the talk of the town as soon as the army stays put in their honorable barracks.

Consequent upon what I saw on moving around the city of Lagos, and the troubling news that Maroko, a booming shantytown in Lagos had been bulldozed, I wrote the following ditty:

Neither the annals of the city of Lagos
Nor the annals of the Lagos State
Would be complete without a reference
To your littoral geography.

When the hour came, 1989, the bulldozers
Showed no sign of sympathy
first, it was the bamboo-walled bungalows the
then the adobe bungalows.
Children, stood, helpless, crying
Women, their backs, mounted by leaders
Of tomorrow, stood, helpless, crying
Even men, the sturdy men, whose sturdy hands
Could break the necks of a thousand elephants,
Stood, watching, in tears.

Maroko, a one-time shantytown

Teeming with about one thousand souls
Had suffered demolition like the suffering
Grass where two or more elephants had frayed.

The only landmark after hours of
Order-to-action was the clinic of
A native doctor and the police post
Jammed with heart-rendering complaints
Without a file.

Apart from angers and rivers of tears
The bulldozers carried out their orders
Without a hitch. But as nightfall brought
The market women to their long-established pitch
A hitch was unavoidable: 'Lords' messengers,
go away: go away with your bulldozers.
"Leave us alone—in peace. You cannot bulldoze
The fingers, the staple foods, that feed you
Everyday before you're fed with the order
To uproot our roofless pitches."

The bulldozers left them in peace.
Some of them though became boat people
But they made sure they sold their
Staple macrobiotic foods everyday, open-air markets.

For months, neither the market women's chats
Nor the talking drums could be made clarion and meaningful
Without adieux Maroko—with tears
Dinning in the ears of young and old!

The Myths of the Coffee Boys which was initially published as The Coffee Boys in 1986 was republished in 1989 by the Development News. It was republished at a time when the Africans in Diaspora in Europe were already tired of carrying the burdens of injustice upon their heads. And Apartheid

181

happened to be one of those areas where people were heavy-laden: where burdens of injustice thrive with abandoned impertinence. In the book, a young schoolgirl cries to the United Nations to trash injustice born out of Apartheid, racism, slavery and colonization, adding that our so-called civilization is mocking the world.

The general mission of *The Myths of the Coffee Boys* (and Girls) is to employ LOVE of mass destruction to destroy evils or agents of Apartheid policy, racism, colonialism, slavery and all forms of inhumanity around the world.

The trashing of these immoral behaviors did not happen oh—Lord—did not happen until 1989 when the Berlin walls were crumbling down as the walls of the Apartheid policy were falling apart in 1990. LOVE has triumphed. Since then I realize that there is nothing LOVE cannot do or achieve, that the Creator has created the world with love and tied humanity (using the strength of gossamer) together with LOVE.

It was December 1989. Before it became a past memory, I chanced to read "The Seven Habits of Highly Effective People" by Stephen L. Covey. On page 36 of the book, he had the following to ruminate upon: "In all of life, there are sequential stages of growth and development. A child learns how to turn over, to sit up, to crawl, and then to walk and run. Each step is important and each one takes time. No step can be skipped. Having read it, I sat up properly and said to myself that I must start this journey of becoming a writer like a child, approaching the sequential stages of my growth and development step by step.

Added to the above, Covey said, *"Writing distills, crystallizes and clarifies the thought."* These seven words actually spur, inspire and enlighten me and I began to sharpen my tongue and gather my pen and paper. Certainly, my search for what will make me a writer has become a desideratum, and to find it is a task that must be done—methodologically—rather than with might and main. Additionally, and as part of Covey's philosophy of education, his heuristic method has gratified my thirst for knowledge: absolute knowledge needed to be a writer.

With those italicized seven words, I began to imbibe the fundamentals that an imaginative literature which is a fountain-head of pleasure (like music) rather than information, nourishes the human emotions, reaffirms the present and reconstructs the future.

No matter what calling one might have, Covey's book has a message for one. It is like a handbook for anyone desiring to pursue any career-goal. Its universal message touches the general public as well as the academia. This might be one of the cardinal reasons why the book is favored by thirty-nine people who reviewed it, praising it rather lavishly.

World of Poetry: In 1990, there were advertisements upon advertisements about the coming together of poets around the world, and for the first time. The organizers put together a lot of energy, ideas and time in sending out flyers, convincing the world that poets should come and attend a conference of poets in Las Vegas—from the last week of August to the first week of September, 1990. In addition, there were beautifully designed cum decorated certificates, diplomas and trophies to be won, and even cash prizes in thousands. After thinking it over and over, ruminating on the pros and cons of leaving my family alone for two weeks, I told my better half that I would attend the conference, convincing her that as a poet I had what it took to be one of the luck cash prize winners.

So I boarded a plane bound for Amsterdam and from Amsterdam to Las Vegas, via Los Angeles. I got to my Hilton hotel room a night before the event started. Breakfast the following morning, and this was followed by registration. The hall was huge, full of poets from around the world who had come to attend the world conference of poets otherwise known as the Convention of World Poetry. They (like me) were all looking for recognition and prizes. Everyone had the burning hope of winning at least a thousand dollars.

After having the chance to read a poem: after the dinner and the flamboyant preparation for the poetry dance of the century, which followed the announcement of what seemed to be the lucky prize winners, I went back to my hotel room at Hilton with a Certificate and what looked to be a gold-plated trophy— feeling more dejected than being disappointed. I was expecting more, like many poets who had expressed their disappointments in frowns and words.

Moving from one hotel to the other, in order to beat down the cost of staying in the city of Las Vegas, the Entertainment Capital of the World, I began to nurse the feeling of wasting my time, believing and thinking that my attending the conference without a cash reward was not worth the effort. In fairness, and admitting the reality without a hiccup, I my coming to attend such a huge gathering of writers from all walks of life makes me a step closer to be a writer, for reading is good and writing is creative.

Today, it appears to me that the thingummy/thingamabob organizer must have used his chicanery to cheat the world— making himself rich at the expense of the unwary poets who were seriously looking for recognition of their labor.

Nineteen Ninety-One: One of those things I will continue to remember even if my immortality is reverted to mortality seems to be a prophecy when the news reached the ears of the world in Europe that Magic had contacted the virus of the incurable disease, called HIV/AIDS. I did not know that United States basketball player could be so popular in Europe. His name even became unstoppably popular after it had been announced that he had been afflicted with the deadly disease.

Every nook and cranny of the unprepossessing city of Vienna was formatted in fear. Fear turned itself into a hob-goblin and the imp turned itself into death and death was pointing to mastabas. Condoms quickly flooded the markets and sex became a luxury without a condom. Makers of condoms suddenly became increased the number of their bank accounts.

Would there be a solution, a remedy? No, was the answer. Why? Because the disease is sprouting from an African guenon: that any disease, caught from animal, and tormenting the world like Mephistopheles must be blamed on the animal kingdom and only the educated lycanthropes can effectively do this. All the above was discussed among my friends and acquaintances on reading a newspaper advising the public how to choose their sex partners, at the end of the meeting of the African Student Union, held at Afro-Asian Institute, Vienna.

"What a shame, he is going to die," said Lola, wrinkling his brows.

"Why?" I riposted.

"The disease is incurable, Yemi. When one contacts it, he/she will die and Magic is going to die."

"I don't think so. I don't think Magic is going to die. If Creator-Philosopher God is my witness, Magic will not die." I kept repeating this until silence separated both of us.

Low and behold, our good humored Magic is still alive today. This gratifies my soul and makes me remember a writer-friend of mine who asserts that most writers are unsung prophets. How I wished I could be one of those in the coterie so that I could speak in tongues of different lingua francas, understood only be the disciples of the Son of Man.

Chapter Thirty

The Departure of the Pearl of the Family

In 1992, the saddest news in almost seventeen years shook the four walls of my fate when the news came that my mother, the pearl of the family died in her sleep. The sad news before this occurred in 1975 when I lost the pretty Maria, the eldest of the siblings. I have none of Maria's photos, yet her milk of kindness and charisma stick to my memory—refreshed everyday like the days of oral literature. Could anything else be sadder—as my beautiful nonagenarian mother—breaking the walls of immortality—leaving—has left to meet her husband who left in 1970, a score year and two ago? Yes, something else could be sadder. Here it is. The news of my mother's death was the saddest as the 20th century was preparing day and night to yield unconditionally to 21st century.

Breaking down before my spouse was not an answer. She could feel that I was grieving but she could not feel the heart of her husband who had lost the pearl of the family whose members are over two thousand.

Going to bed that night was not the first thing in my mind. My aim was to stay awake, grieving all night long. But the night, with its heavy club, knocked me almost unconscious to the bed. I was not dazed. I lay on the bed looking toward the ceiling as though the spirit of my mother would descend to comfort me. My eyes welled up with tears, soddening the area which my somatic trunk had occupied without the knowledge of my second half who could not enjoy to the full her own share of a snoring night-sleep. I burst into a passion of sobs many times. As I was relishing a sweet dream, the symbol of immortality (i-m-m) appeared to me. Why wondering the reason behind its appearance, the Supreme Being showed up his awe-inspiring presence.

Consequently, and without abandoning me in the sea of helplessness, he said, "My son, I know your desire to be an immortal on the surface of the earth. I know your desire to be a centenarian. Which one of the two do you want me to give you?"

Looking like a child on the laps of its mother, I said with a confident grin, "Father, give me both. Both are good. Both are under your auspices."

Putting his index finger on his right cheek, he said, "You are qualified to have one of the two but not both."

"Qualified?"

"Yes, you're qualified, my son."

"What makes me qualified, O Father of heaven and earth?"

"What qualifies you is because you are my creature in whom I am pleased."

"If pleasure is what you derive from your son, despite his bad-eyed behaviors, I will, with your full-fledge leverage, your chapter and verse, your earthly and heavenly authority, choose to become a centenarian who will climb the ladder of invisibility (like Elijah) to your eternal abode of perpetual happiness."

"You have it."

No sooner he uttered that than he disappeared. No sooner he vanished than I genuflected on the bed and offered a prayer of thanksgiving to the king of kings, and the lord of lords.
Standing up gingerly, I headed towards the bathroom-mirror and discovered that my eyes were badly swollen and reddish like the eyes of a pound-for-pound or a blow-for-blow street brawler or prize pugilist. Thank God, my nose remains normal: the weeping did not turn it into a pug nose. I wept like a child who turned his stubbornness and recalcitrance into a *moral obedience*
188

on a moral high ground, having received spanking on a daily basis—before breakfast. All this grieving: all this crying and sobbing would not make a change. What could have made a difference is that if the immortal Creator-Philosopher Olorun had agreed to give my mother of an exceptional beauty and pulchritude another chance to enjoy a life enriched with peace, spiritual wellness, good health and blessedness.

The participants/students of the Institute of Creative Writing noticed my crestfallen visage and they did not need a magic wand to know that something uglier than a clout and more important than the ritual grains of paradise had shaken my manhood and put a dent as well as a question mark in my God-given immortality.

It took me a few days before I could come up with what memento I had to give to my mother. That memento is called:

Mother and Mothers

I did not know it was so
Burdensome to become a parent
And now I realize and kvetch
Like a captious preceptor
Forgetting all those wrongs
My pearly mother had borne with
Understanding, love and patience.

She had borne me in her womb
For nine lunar moons
She had catered for me day and night
She had shielded me from the aggression
Of the world, mosquitoes inclusive
Bed & back wetting, never forgotten
She had succored me and cured me
With only the herbs in our backyard bush.
While thanking her and other mothers
Around the world, whose children
Had trodden the path, similar to mine

189

I also wish her glories and peace
As she is journeying from this mortal world
To the Pearly Gates, the new world
Where the sun rises and never sets
Shining endlessly.

Mother and Mothers
May your days be glorious, sweet
Tempest-free, trouble-free
Sunny, blissful and peaceful.

Chapter Thirty-One

Creator-Philosopher Olodumare, My Spiritual Teacher

Three things happened almost simultaneously in 1991, a year before the loss of the pearl of the family. These three things are the three books, published the same year. These are *Studying Creative Writing in Nigeria, The Writers and Politics* and *The Literary Philosophy for the Year 2000.*

In reviewing *Studying Creative Writing in Nigeria,* the publisher (Merlin Books) has the following to say: "This well-planned and highly useful course on creative writing is, as its title suggests, aimed mainly at Nigerians, although it could also be of interest to peoples of other nationalities. Including information on the origin of creative writing, types of writing, critical approaches and literary terms, the book is a most comprehensive and interesting one.

"The author first started writing at the University of Graz in 1978. By the time he moved to Vienna, he had already established himself as the only writer who could succeed in a land where the language of communication is neither Yoruba nor English.

"In 1983, he set up a summer institute of creative writing to promote research in African literatures.

"In 1987, he was awarded a certificate as an Ambassador of Hope by the Austrian Institute for Professional Research.

"Twice in 1990 he was given the title of golden poet by the World of Poetry, and received two certificates of merit as well as a golden trophy. In the space of just seven years, he has produced over forty published and unpublished works. *CREATIVE WRITING IN NIGERIA,* being his most recent work."

Reading is good. Writing is Creative. These six words with a total of thirty letters were already a household word when the Institute of Creative Writing was established in 1983. And by the time, *Studying Creative Writing in Nigeria* was published in 1991, **Becoming a Writer** has already formed the warp and weft of my being. I think I can do it even if I find no big-time publisher to *discover* me.

If the review of the publisher has anything to portray as success, it is a feeling of *reading is good while writing is creative* that carries the foundation upon which that success rests.

The Writers and Politics was published at the heels of Desert Storm that began in 1991. It chronicles the world and shows how the writers have failed to persuade the politicians to always desist from making wars that do not support the creation, the wellness and the enlightenment of mankind, as well as the civilization of the mind, heart and soul.

The Literary Philosophy for the Year 2000, published the same year as *Studying Creative Writing in Nigeria,* bears an entirely different dimension. Written and described as a roman a these (thesis novel.) It is designed to encourage women's participation in the political, economic and social process. Equally, it is written to correct the wrong the general public has noticed among the leaders. Plus the fact that it encourages the government and the governed to be united by ties of consanguinities.

Looking at it from a critical point of view and putting into intellectual consideration what Professor Jeremy Hawthorn, author of STUDYING THE NOVEL, (1985); has postulated, the roman a these is supposed to be a simple and uncomplicated narrative. He referred to Harriet Beecher Stowe's UNCLE TOM's CABIN (1852) which he said attacked the institution of slavery in the United States of America.

However, Hawthorn pointed out that not all novels that attack can be termed a roman a these. An example of this is Thomas Hardy's *JUDY THE OBSCURE* (1896). Although the novel undeniably dumps some attack upon certain social conventions, it is too complex to be called a thesis novel.

Another work, too complex to be regarded a roman a these is THE INTERPRETERS (1965) by Wole Soyinka, 1986 Nobel Prize Winner in Literature.

Apart from being a thesis novel, I had the idea of writing *The Literary Philosophy for the Year 2000* as I crisscrossed European countries. During my crisscrossing, I continued to come across many European philosophers in my reading. One night, I prayed Olodumare to open my eyes to Yoruba Philosophy. The upshot of my prayers gave birth to the book. The book is like a wake-up call to Yoruba scholars and intellectuals in search of American and European philosophy—asking them why carrying coal to Enugu while we have enough coal in Enugu? The minor premise made vivid and unequivocal to me is that Nigerians have what it takes to reach the crest of the mount, for if the ancient and the unbeatable terra-cotta arts could make it to the top without a formal education, the Nigerians with an archives of degree, fellowship and research diplomas can also refuse to stay complacently at the foot of the mount.

Chapter Thirty-Two

The Afrormosia is Leaving

As months, weeks and days passed by, so also Studying Creative Writing in Nigeria passed into the hands of curious connoisseurs of world literature. In the spring of 1992, as I was preparing to go to the British Library, my phone rang. I always visited the British and the American Libraries almost on a daily basis. Lifting up the receiver, I said hello and a female voice reciprocated. What followed is a congenial dialogue:

Good morning.

Good morning.

Are you Yemi? The female voice asked.

Yemi: Yes I am.

Good morning.

Good morning.

Joe Shobel: Are you Yemi D. Ogunyemi, author of Studying Creative Writing in Nigeria?

Yemi: Yes I am Yemi.

Joe Shobel: Yemi, my name is Joe Shobel (of the Blue Danube Radio), radio producer for the international community in Vienna. A copy of your book has landed in my office. It is a good book. When did you start to write it?

Yemi: I started writing it in 1983 when the Institute of Creative Writing was founded.

Joe Shobel: I am told you are a family man: when did you have the time to write it and other titles to your name?

Yemi: I am a stealer of time. I often steal time from my spouse and children. Without their cooperation and understanding, I could not have written the book, as well as others.

Joe Shobel: Would you mind if the Radio International interviews you about your book?

Yemi: That will be great. I will love it.

Joe Shobel: Do you know where the station is located?

Yemi: I know where the station is. I have been there several times.

Joe Shobel: Okay. I shall be expecting you on Tuesday...Give me a call if anything happens that may prevent you from coming. If that happens, I will set for you another appointment. Okay?

Yemi: Okay.

As early as eighty-thirty on April 25, 1992, Joe received me in her office.

"Sit down and feel at home," said Joe with a spread of perfume and promise on her face.

"Thank you," I said with the smiles of the spring season on my face.

"Yemi, tell me what brought you to write a textbook on Creative Writing?"

"It is my love for Creative Writing that led me to write it. Its research began in 1983 when the Institute of Creative writing was established."

"How will you describe creative writing?"

"Creative Writing is the writing that comes out of imagination. And in my own case, it is conflated with literary philosophy."

"Could you shed some light on literary philosophy?"

"Literary philosophy is the blending of philosophy with literature and autochthonous religion."

"You have a PhD in International Politics, how easy is it to have it replaced with literature?"

"I have forgotten that I have written the book in other area other than politics. But since I don't use politics but literature, I don't think of its importance any longer."

"Where did you carry out its research?"

"Its research was carried out here in Vienna, making use of the American and the British libraries."

"Who are your African authors?"

"They are many. Some of them are Wole Soyinka, Chinua Achebe, Camara Laye, Obi B. Egbuna, D.O. Fagunwa, Ngugi wa Thiong'o, Alex Haley, Maya Angelou."

"And being the first African writer to be awarded Nobel Prize in literature, Wole Soyinka must have greatly inspired you."

"Absolutely. He is my mentor."

"Great. Not long ago, I read about the Festac held in Lagos in 1977. It brought together black people from all over the world. Did you attend it?"

"I did not attend it, unfortunately. But I felt its presence here in Vienna. It is a thing of magnitude. I call it a 'cultural jamboree.' The only people missed during the festival are the blacks from India. I hope they will attend if ever the third one is held, knowing that the first one in Dakar in 1966 and the second in Lagos are both successful."

"When and where will the third one be held?"

"No date and place set yet. However, it is a thing of joy to hear that the Second Black and African Festival of Arts and Culture (Festac) has provided a forum for Africans in Africa and Africans in Diaspora to shed light on the diverse contributions made by Africans since the beginning of man."

"Yemi, is there any part of your book you will like to read?"

"Yes indeed. I will like to read chapter three which is the Origin of Creative Writing."

"Go ahead." She said like a Yoruba woman who refused to attend a party because she did not have the right head-beauty.

"Studying the origin of creative writing, one has to travel back in time. Fictional narrative is as old as mankind. The autobiographical writing of Olaudah Equiano is only two hundred years old. But oral ballads and oral fictional narratives have long been in existence, like a joy-bell in a community fete.

"If my grandfather had lived up till today, he could probably have told me that I would not be able to lift up his narratives, were they written down and kept in a portmanteau. And that is just about my grandfather (among Elders in our compound) whose fictions live till today although I was a kid of a few rainy seasons when he paid the debt of nature.

"If this has been the case, a Department of Oral Literature, Faculty of Folklore, could have since been created at Obafemi Awolowo University, to research deeply into a universe which Divinity-Philosopher Oduduwa was carving before he passed on.

"Whether the family man was a farmer, a fisher, a hunter or a traveling wrestler, he always came back to his compound to relate his epic experiences of successes or failures. The books of D.O. Fagunwa, Amos Tutuola are examples.

"But Nigerian households and glitterati do not pride themselves on narratives and poems alone. The dramas we know today, have their origins in traditional festivals, family and royal entertainments. And this is one of the reasons why Messrs A.B. David, A.G. Onimole, A.A. Layeni and Chief Hubert Ogunde remain exemplars by exploring the family roots and introducing what is now known as a traveling or mobile theater in the country."

That night as I slept, I dreamt seeing a tree, as huge as banyan—leaving gorgeously. The dream was fascinating and the foliage was amazing, incredible. Shortly before I woke up, I saw myself leaving the city of Vienna without my family. The interpretation of the dream was beyond the compass of my comprehension. Thus I wrote the dream on a piece of paper, put it inside an envelope, then under my pillows, hoping my guarding angel would reveal the meaning to me later or sooner.

Before the end of 1992, my spouse, on being misinformed by one of her sisters that I was going to Nigeria to introduce what I have been preaching—introducing and teaching Creative Writing in one of the universities, went surreptitiously to the District Court in Floridsdorf-Vienna and asked the court to sever the tie of our matrimony. The court refused to do so on the grounds that my going to teach in Nigeria was not enough reason to divorce. What I made known to my spouse is that the entire family would be going to America, and not Nigeria.

Weeks later, my mother-in-law enunciated that her daughter could not go to either Nigeria or America due to the inadequacy of her spoken English. The feeling that I had married more than one spouse troubled me—with reference to what my sister-in-law and my mother-in-law were saying. Eventually, they succeeded in convincing the judge that breaking the marriage was good for my spouse.

The cohabitation died like a few—very few I know. The judge, fingers splayed on her table, shook her head helplessly in consolation. Looking tearful like someone who was pinioned by abulia, she did not utter a word. And when she spoke, her words came through teeth glittering in the most courteous and infectious of smiles.

Creating words and ideas is part of Creative Writing. Words and ideas are not always formed at the same time. But that day, I had words and ideas in abundance. Thus I let her know that to err is human and that she had badly erred. I let her know that I could not have come to her court if fairness was not part and parcel of her constitution. Emphatically, I made it known to her that I could not have reacted to her summons if, if.

"If what?" she asked with decorum.

"If I had known that abulia will have a role to play in your judgment." I said in an affected smile, ridiculed by a moue and knitted brows.

I left the courtroom without fully replacing my facial expressions. Even when I entered my car, the expressions were still noticeable till I got home. After my breakfast which was followed by reading **Mandela's Earth and Other Poems** by Wole Soyinka, my face started to glow with enthusiasm as a result of *Reading is Good. Writing is Creative.*

Days later, I was preparing to die spiritually like my parents and then beseech the Supreme Being to give me tenancy at the Pearly Gates—like my parents. But the Creator of the Pearly Gates will never think mortally like me. In separating mortality from immortality, he asked me to die and I died. Consequently, I plunged into the unknown: into the unknown, I resurrected.

As I was preparing to step into the unknown, I had the opportunity to attend a conference on the International Year of the World Indigenous People held in Vienna, on June 8, 1993.

200

At that time, I regarded myself (and I still do) as an aborigine, filling the legendary dots left behind in Ile-Ife (the Garden of Love) by Oduduwa, the theanthropic primogeniture of the Yoruba people. Had I had a paper to deliver that day, I could have replaced myth with facts and then print them out.

In February 1994, I left for Avadh University, India for my Doctor of Letters. This was after I had completed my PhD program in Nigerian/African Literature at Debrecen University, Hungary.

After I had submitted every requirement for my Doctor of Letter at Avadh University, I left for Vienna to see my kids. After a few weeks of ensconcing, I left for Harvard University, Department of African-American Studies, as Associate Research Fellow, on May 31, 1994. Here, at this institution of higher learning where everything is discoursed except immortality, where a sylph flibbertigibbet who is neither albino nor *albina* (albina being the feminine opposite of albino) with a penumbra of lies upon her forehead, tried to tarnish my family record of honesty by backbiting me. But before she could be too harmful to the institution and the community, she was transferred by forces beyond her control.

Before the end of that year, I had the opportunity to attend Henry Louis Gates Junior's reading of the *Colored People* at the old African Meeting Place in Boston. Like the title of this work, *Becoming a Writer*, Professor Gates Junior has written the memoirs like a novel that reflects his formative years. For some reason which is not clear to me, the reading was not well-attended. However, the book was a bestseller in its own right.

The more I think of immortality, the more I think of Becoming a Writer. The thought of this, combined, makes me a happy-go-lucky creature of a man. And more often than not, I tremble with happiness.

Book II

Chapter Thirty-Three

Treading Upon The Land Of Dreams

An idea which I had in mind which led to two of my writing projects on stepping upon the American soil is to complete a *bildungsroman*. The other one is to complete a Dictionary of Literary Terms which I started in 1983. My idea is to compile these literary terms and nomenclatures in such a way as to separate Elizabethan English from American English. I wanted to conjecture, for example, why the past tense of travel should be spelt in two different ways or variants— *travelled/traveled*. Two years ago, I abandoned the idea of completing the project due to the vicissitudes of life.

In 1995, on moving from Cambridge to Boston, an American princess who is originally from Jamaica met me in a Pentecostal Church, pastored by Matthew Babalola. After six moons of courtship, we went into the rituals of engagement and consequently into marriage—November 8, 1995; the very year I set up Diaspora Press of America.

In 1997, a year before ***Introduction to Yoruba Philosophy, Religion and Literature*** was published, I chanced to meet a prolific Nigerian writer who has the gab of writing fiction and poetry. His name is Sunny. When asked if American publishers are encouraging writers from the developing countries, his answer was an affirmative no.

Paraphrastically, he said, "How could the British publishers disown their own —their fellow Commonwealth citizens? In the 1960s, they encouraged us to write so that they could publish whatever we wrote. But today they have left us in the lurch. They never encourage us to write any longer, let alone publish what we write. What's going on?"

Both of us seemed not to know what was going us. Thus I pouted, and he pouted, shaking his head like someone hearing the BBC news that a trust-worthy friend had stabbed his sworn friend on the back.

As a result of a day-to-day research done on Yoruba ways of life, with emphasis on Ile –Ife whose two variants are *The House of Love* and *The Garden of Love*, respectively, I completed writing Introduction to Yoruba Philosophy, Religion and Literature in 1998. The same year, it was published by Athelia Henrietta Press, New York. The book is a sequel to Literatures of the African Diaspora whose research took me to the six continents of the world in search of the avant-garde writers and people of the African descent.

Introduction to Yoruba Philosophy, Religion and Literature gives birth to a number of critics who say that it is not full enough. One of my replies is that Yoruba culture and everything Yoruba stands for is on the rise. And because it is on the rise, cannot be complete under a cover of just three titles. For discoursing about Ile-Ife alone, one has to write a tome of a book to satisfy every critic. Thus Introduction to Yoruba Philosophy, Religion Literature is the beginning of a larger aspect of the Yoruba ways of life, while the present is an eye-opener.

Published simultaneously with the above textbook by the same publisher is ***The Covenant of the Earth.*** It deals with the religion and philosophy of the Yoruba people from a narrative perspective. And who are the creatures involved here? They are the deities—the gods and goddesses, most of whom have been demythologized as Divinity-Philosophers. In a narrative form, the author tells among other salient points how these gods and goddesses decided to leave their heavenly abode for the earthly abode, thus fulfilling their covenant with the earth.

Why Introduction to Yoruba Philosophy, Religion and Literature was published before Literature of the African Diaspora is that I was incarcerated by indecision at that time—placing my principles over expediencies and vice versa. Luckily, I do the right thing, for many of the Africans in Diaspora who are straining at the leash to read more about the Yoruba philosophy, religion and literature have the opportunity to read it. The book was published in the nick of time.

At this juncture, I have to refer to Ijapa again whom I first referred to in Chapter Three. *Introduction to Yoruba Philosophy, Religion and Literature* is the book I was writing when he first appeared to me in 1988.

According to the Yoruba long pedigree of legends, Ijapa is the folk hero and the fabled protagonist of antiquity in Yoruba folktales. He is an active creature, an unpredictable endomorph that ever lived. He is nasty as he is upstanding: a boisterous culture vulture, half genius, half doltish: a philosopher who can upload and download when least expected. No Yoruba folktale could be told with a yawn and a stretch without the presence of Ijapa, depicted and characterized as a tortoise. Ijapa is the past-master with a golden passé-partout. He is both the punch-line and the cliffhanger of a story. A story could be sweet or bitter because of him. Sometimes he would present himself as the sinner or as the harbinger of confusion. Sometimes he would present himself as the saint and harbinger of wellness and immortality. (Mr.) Ijapa exemplifies perfection. He is a know-all magic realist, a flibbertigibbet, a prestidigitator who could force a virgin hen to lay eggs.

As I was contemplating of becoming a full time writer in 1983, the idea of carrying out some research on Ijapa pushed me to the wall, to the cul-de-sac where I commenced to cudgel my brains.

My initial finding is that Ijapa is a doppel-ganger, a creature that holds a visaed passport of double personality. My first question is: Why should a creature be both human and amphibian? The question led me to another ladder of research in which I discovered that in all the oral and written legends of the Yoruba people, miraculously and mysteriously chosen to be the children of Creator-Philosopher Olodumare, and abandoned in a land flowing with milk and honey, known as Ile-Ife or the

Garden of Love, no indication that an amphibian in the name of a tortoise was created during the days and hours of creation, under the chapter and verse of Divinity-Philosopher Obatala. Who among the deities must have changed his/her name to Ijapa? Why must a chosen people allow a tortoise to take charge of their house?

The upstairs questions troubled me like someone forgotten in the realm of phantasmagoria where oxymoron is the order of the day: bitterness versus sweetness, positive versus negative, happiness versus sorrow, laughing versus crying, pursued me in my sleepless nights. The first time he appeared to me (like a changeling) was when I was writing *Introduction to Yoruba Philosophy, Religion and Literature*. He stood on my way like a conjurer who had the whole world under his conjure. On penetrating his obstruction, he said to me, "The door shall be open to every soul that knocks."

The second time he appeared to me (like a revenant) was during a gloaming—when I had just finished writing *The Political Philosophy of Wole Soyinka and Other Narratives*. He said to me in a basso profundo, "Whosoever seeks shall find," and disappeared as quickly as he had appeared.

The third time, he appeared to me, he was an omniscient narrator, wearing a dashiki whose front was carrying a symbol of terra-cotta, while its back was carrying an emblem of a philosophical mask of the king of Ile-Ife. It was during the writing of *The Serpent's Tails*, which was later replaced by *Twice Anagram*. He said to me, "If you don't ask, how can you find what you are looking for?" I told him I always asked myself why I have not been able to put a smile on the lips of every creature.

Guffawing like a sarsaparilla drinker, he said he was tired of seeing people misusing the opportunities Creator-Philosopher Olodumare had given them. He disclosed that he is a human being created in the image and the likeness of Creator-Philosopher Olodumare.

Stroking his philosophical beard, he enunciated, "I am no skeleton, dragged out of its shadow to dance a bone dance in the middle of the leading strings. Those who do not believe my humanness are not attacking me but my shadow."

In addition to the supra, he enjoined me to implore and caution the Africans in Africa and Africans in Diaspora not to let the grass grow under their feet in the 21st century.

While bidding me farewell, he prayed me to have faith, and to try to make use of my sixth sense. He adjured me to bruit it about that he is not a reptile but a human being with flesh and bones like Divinity-Philosopher Oduduwa, the primogenitor and pioneer of Yoruba philosophy.

The research has shown that this folk hero, called Ijapa is God's messenger. He is also ubiquitous and immortal. The amaranth of immortality was bestowed on him by the Creator himself. Because of this, he is ubiquitous with the power to act as omniscient narrator. But not all immortals are ubiquitous. The bottom line is that no one becomes a story teller (oral or written story teller) without the knowledge of Ijapa. Passing from one generation to another, oral stories are indispensable. What makes them folktales are the variants of the stories that can be told over time and space—with Ijapa, invariably acting as the protagonist. Essentially, to be regarded a folktale, a story must be told over and over again. I know Ijapa but he knows me more than I know him.

Ijapa's Chant:
An edifying chatterbox
Claimed without a hearing
My obeisance
Made by your patriarchate.

Paradoxical sleeper
Between a snore and a sleep
Purchaser of aces sourcing from the
Realm of acme
Pedigreed field of roses
My obeisance I pay.

Dispenser of reasons for victories
Mythicized common sense
Fabled prestidigitator of antiquity
A recalcitrant protagonist
Whose deuteragonists left
No choice but pray and amen
My obeisance I pay.

Unpredictable folklorist and diviner
Fretting under the axe of guillotine
A nexus betwixt Ifalogy and Ifadom
A doppelganger between
Folktales and folk memories
This is my obeisance
Charmed before your carapace.

Escapades stunted betwixt
Fictions and nonfictions
The rise and fall of the tide
A cock without a crow
A trickster fabled in paronomasia
A sponger in the house of hospitality
A reifier and feigner in a famished land
A passé-partout to the crises unsolved
A denouement for mysteries
Legend of comedy for manners
My obeisance I make.

A lotus-eater in a lotus land of feints
An ageless fire-eater
An indispensable friend or foe
Pray never to become your dill
Even in the Day of Immortality—Sunday
For all your dwelling cowries of mythopoeia
My obeisance, pray, I pay.

The creative energy of his characteristics has made me write *Studying Creative Writing in Nigeria, Introduction to Yoruba Philosophy, Religion and Literature, Literatures of the African Diaspora*. These are the three main titles, pointing to me the vista leading to my Becoming a Writer. Those three textbooks teach me the following:

Never a day without a line
Be bold
Be curious
Be painstaking
Be confident
Always fall in love with words.

Of course there are a few other titles which have emboldened me to become a quality writer (not just a jejune one)—all of them reminding me that reading is good, while writing is creative, divine, sublime and spiritually uplifting.

While carrying out my research on those literary works, I came across race issues, accentuated by *Race Matters* by Professor Cornell West which did enlighten me indeed. In some of my meetings with Africans in Diaspora, I have discussed something like this with them: After many years of research on race issues, the need for mankind to have a single skin color, **brown**, becomes more imperative than ever. The researchers have noticed that one can only be brown, browner, brownest, for as there no one who is as black as charcoal, so also there is no one who is as white as snow. Why then the fuss and the cutthroat restlessness after decades of our civilization? Brown is the color from the womb. Unequivocally, the skin classification has been the handwork of colonialist/imperialist etymologists cum ethnologists—over 500 fat years.

The researchers are aware that the multi-racial wars, clashes, conflicts, prejudices, conjectures and disparagements in regions such as Africa, Americas, Australasia and Europe were caused by the colonialist/imperialist etymologists/ethnologists who partitioned the skin-color into black, white and yellow. Who in this present century is not aware that Nelson Mandela was incarcerated for 27 years because of skin color?

Now then, in order to make the world a better place to dwell, as we approach the year 2000, the researchers are suggesting one skin color, **brown**, for humanity. They are also suggesting that ethnic identities be referenced according to their geographical locations. Thus the *colorless world* will be referenced like this: Africans, Americans, Asians and Europeans.

Furthermore, in a heterogeneous country like America, the references will be Africans-Americans, Asian-Americans, Euro-Americans, Latin-Americans, Native Americans and so and so forth. Brown is a decolonized color and so it makes the world to stick together like brothers and sisters (like a natural gum), oblivious and regardless of what is worn over our skeletons.

Today, I can't tell with certainty whether the whole wide world has been decolonized. Nor can I say with a cross over my heart if slavery has been wiped out from the surface of the earth. What I can say is that the cutthroat matters will continue until a spiritual world is born. We are in trouble and we shall continue to be in trouble because we are trouble-makers/shooters despite many decades of civilization.

Chapter Thirty-Four

Leave a Little Bit for Omoneye

Summer **1999 Writing Retreat:** Summer 1999 was another chapter of sadness. This was when I was having a three-month literary retreat on a secluded hilly residential area in Waltham, a town, about fifteen miles from Boston/Cambridge. After spending two months there, the sad news came from Nigeria that my youngest brother, Omoneye (popularly called Taylor) had passed away. The news saddened and angered me and I proceeded to question my Creator why he should allow one to die when one is not yet an octogenarian or a centenarian, for example. Did God hear me? Yes, so I thought. But I could not change anything that is in the interest of the Giver of Life and Death. Needless to say that his death put many dents on the invisible dashiki of immortality that I have been wearing— fortunately. He was three years my junior at primary school. A Jehovah Witness by faith, he was like my liaison officer between Nigeria and America before he died. I missed him sorely—still missing him—and my face, still as long as a fiddle, even if I am as fit as a fiddle.

One unforgettable joke made by one of my seniors in primary school is "Leave a little bit for Omoneye." The jocular sentence was uttered during a lunch time in 1957. It was a plea. Seeing that the older and bigger boys were running ahead of Omoneye and me to the lunch hall where every individual kept his meal and where other meals could be devoured without regard to the owner, I shrieked out, "Leave a little bit for Omoneye. Thank God, the hungry mouths heeded my plea. And I was glad that they did. Since then, the humor has remained a "literary flashback," refreshing my memory and whetting my appetite nostalgically, not only for those macrobiotic foods of 1950s but also whetting my appetite to see my younger brother.

Chapter Thirty-Five

A Verbal Reasoning Material Writer

In July 25, 1999 while dabbling in nondescript intellectual and scholarly fields of interest, I came across an announcement in the Times Literary Supplement that American Institutes for Research (AIR) in Washington D.C. needed writers to develop test material for the Medical College Admission Test (MCAT.)

Without allowing my pen to bear me out, I wrote a short letter to the American Institutes, "lying" that as a writer, I would like to become one of the writers needed. This was a day after I saw the announcement.

On September 23rd 1999, the following reply, written and signed by Dr. Laureen Martin, Medical College Admission Test Editor, was received:

The American Institutes for Research (AIR) has been awarded the contract to develop test material for the Medical College Admission Test (MCAT.) We are pleased to inform you that the Association of American Medical Colleges (AAMC) has approved your application to write verbal reasoning material for the MCAT.

Before I can offer you a writing assignment, AIR needs two completed forms from you (enclosed.) The first is a confidentiality agreement, the purpose of which is to ensure the security of potential test material. It states that you agree not to disclose information about the MCAT to anyone unconnected with the project and not to contribute in any way to a test preparation service—for example, Princeton Review courses—for five years from the formal termination of your agreement with us. The second is a summary of professional information.

Your completion of a third enclosed form, Personal Data Sheet for All MCAT contractors is optional. Its purpose is to attest to our efforts to maintain equity in employment. We ask that you sign and return this form, whether or not you choose to complete it.

Please mail the three forms to AIR in the envelope provided. After receiving them, I will phone you to arrange an initial assignment and I will send you a writer's guide with complete instructions. The enclosed statement, Writing Verbal Reasoning Items for the MCAT, summarizes the task of writers. I hope that you'll enjoy the challenges of this process, and I look forward with pleasure to working with you.

On October 8, 1999, I appended my signature to an agreement by MCAT to respect the following seven points: One: Every writing assignment will be accepted by the item writer by telephone or e-mail1 and confirmed in writing by the editor.

Two: All work submitted to the American Institute for Research (AIR) under this agreement will be written solely by the item writer (the person signing this agreement), will meet the standards of AIR and of the Association of American Medical Colleges (AAMC), as stated in a writer's guide provided to the item writer, and will be sent to AIR by the agreed date.

Three: The item writer will not disclose information about the structure, emphasis, or composition of the MCAT or about material submitted to AIR to anyone outside of AIR or the project staff of AAMC. Furthermore, the item writer will not disclose his/her role in MCAT item development or use any material or information he/she has acquired as an item writer in preparing or teaching any class or in advising any student.

Four: The item writer affirms that he/she has had no connection with—e.g, has not been employed by a test preparation service in the past five years.

Five: The item writer agrees to have no connection with—e.g., not to be employed by a test preparation service for five years from the formal termination of this agreement.

Six: All material submitted under this agreement will be the exclusive property of AAMC. The item writer will make no further use of submitted material without written permission from AAMC.

Seven: The AIR may describe the item writer's training and experience in reports to AAMC.

Becoming an item writer is not the same as becoming a creative writer. This is my impression on seeing the assignment before me. The assignment is about 500 pages. Each item has four response alternatives, one of which can be confirmed as correct by information in the passage and the others plausible and syntactically similar distracters.

The entire assignment was as though I was in an English/Linguistic class where grammatically every sentence has to be well constructed, taken into consideration regular, irregular forms of nouns, verbs and adjectives: comparative and superlative forms of adjectives: countable and uncountable nouns: as well as the subject, accusative, dative, genitive, nominative and objective cases. I think I am more than certain that I will one day become a writer—turning myself into a mystic green plant, deriving the energy of the sunlight for my growth. Indeed I am a mystic green plant and no pollution will stop me from growing. All I need, indispensable it is, is the energy of the sunlight. Period.

A book in hand, I nearly fell head-long as I stumbled while descending my hilly literary retreat one late morning in 2000. On regaining my balance, the declivity led me to a runnel. Here three ideas were gestated which were quickly put into fruition with scenarios that were in the process of formation.

Chapter Thirty-Six

Soon After Becoming an Item Writer

The first idea was to write a novel which I began to write. The second idea was to write a book about Wole Soyinka's political philosophy which I did. The third was to write a book on *ifetherapy*, the ancient massage therapy, peculiar to the Atlantic Yoruba people.

It is an ambitious to think of writing three books at the same time. I thought many times of blaming the afflatus for putting the ideas before me. However, in summer of 2001, I completed *The Political Philosophy of Wole Soyinka and Other Narratives* and *Path to Ifetherapy and Its Healing Poems*. *The Political Philosophy of Wole Soyinka and Other Narratives* is a dedication for Wole Soyinka for being the first African to be awarded Nobel Prize in literature and for pioneering a political culture and literary philosophy. Paragraph 3 of its Foreword reads, "Additionally, African philosophy will invariably be a limb borrowed from European philosophy if our researchers do not discourse, emphasize and bring to the fore the folk philosophy, the people's philosophy, known long before the advent of the occupiers."

Path to Ifetherapy and Its Healing Poems does not only use the application of hands to massage—to healing the body and soul but also the power of words. The WORD is the most important phenomenon on earth, and in heaven, the superlative will remain unchanged. With reference to Ifa-Ife, the Book of Enlightenment, embodying philosophy, literature and religion, the WORD is a sine qua non. When properly used, it gives birth to peace, happiness and unconditional love, even good health and semi-immortality.

219

Chapter Thirty-Seven

The Ground under My Feet

Understanding that I was born into a vale of the 20th century—full of hardships, sorrows, woes, wars (1st and 2nd World Wars) and rumors of wars, I was so enthused to learn that on January 1, 2001, a new century in a novel millennium would be born: believing man would eventually emerge from the valley of darkness into a glade of light, dignity, probity, peace and love.

All the good things that could happen must happen to occupy my mind, not least the bliss that I am able to complete and publish two books in the same year. This good feeling rejuvenated me from head to toe. I was trembling with happiness, so bright and visible that it could turn the night into day. It was as though I was atop a mount of transfiguration where the Holy Spirit had taken over my corporeal being. I was overwhelmed with *running feelings*—feeling too sensitive and too touchy to express. These feelings were to live forever—so I thought, like the amaranth of immortality, now sprouting. But on September 11, 2001 when these good feelings have firmly established themselves, a monstrous demon without respect for lives and status symbols struck. The destruction of the World Trade Center, New York, was an eye-sore—people died in hundreds. The ground beneath my feet trembled as if Armageddon had come to claim the mortal world. The bag-eyed destruction made me feel my literary works, simply a run-of-the-mill.

(Let's not forget that during the summer months of the same year, I was stunned and made dumb when I saw on the screen how the bushes, the grasses, the woods and the forests in a certain part of California were set ablaze, smokes rising high into the firmament and forming cloud-scrapers, and the blaze causing millions of dollars contain. I knelt down one evening and asked Creator-Philosopher Olodumare to protect from the blaze all my black and white brothers and sisters living in the state of California.)

According to my father, fire when burning, is like an angry warlord, destroying all in its path without regard to life and property. Why a wild fire in a prosperous California when the Trade Centre in a wealthy New York had just been razed to the ground? How did the fire come about? I was made to understand that the bushes, the grasses, the woods and forests were set ablaze by a demonic pyromaniac. I was helpless, not knowing what to say. But I murmured the following to myself: if a demonic pyromaniac could torment the sole super-power in the world, what will happen if it turns to a non-super-power country and releases its demonic venom?

It seemed the dead in their mass graves—men, women, young and old were the souls causing the ground to shake beneath my feet. On the other hand, I felt as though the pollution above my head, caused by man, on earth, would fall upon my head, knocking me down flat, helplessly. There were so many imageries of palpability and impalpability as there were ironies and metaphors of people running helter-skelter—crying and rejoicing, dying and awaking, et cetera. In what presented itself as a vision, or was it hallucination, I beheld dozens of people trooping out of their homes with bags on their backs, and padding purposelessly like swagmen. The entire world was a hay of confusion: in a topsy-turvy manner.

Seeing those twin landmarks in the metropolis of New York burning during my breakfast was sorrowful as it was scary. It was as though the whole world was on fire. I rubbed my eyes several time to ensure I was not day-dreaming, for it was my duty to make sure that nature was not playing hanky-panky on me. Gluing myself to the television for hours, hearing, pondering over what the newscasters were saying, I was convinced beyond any quandary that nature was playing a trick on me. This was an utter destruction as it was a mini destruction when my parents' houses were gutted down in 1956—forty-five years ago. That incident is in a book already and this one must also be in a book—feeling as if my parents' houses were burning again. If this feeling is right, it is because human beings are interdependent—what affects A affects B (Darby and Joan)—directly or indirectly. What affects the nose affects the eyes—directly or indirectly.

That month of September, I didn't know when I badly injured my right wrist: thank God that I am ambidextrous. At the end of that year, when the smoke and eddies of combustion and confusion were settling down, I improvised the following poetry:

Victory over Devil
Before:
The night, a birth to the 11th day of September
Out of the ordinary and special
A joyful day in gestation
To be redeemed during the crepuscular hour
But the Devil has wrought its wrath
Upon the unwary world—WTC:
In thousands people perished.

When a Devilish buffoon
On a destructive rampage goes
Sanity will devise a means
To deter his buffoonery.

After:

We go from weakness to strength
From statics to dynamics
From crassitude to sapience
From inactive to proactive
From hate to love
From disunity to unity.

Nothing but a paean to utter
If all has been uttered
All must be altered
For our samskara is one—one salvation
May the terrorists not
Turn it into yaw
This is not the time to yawn.

Footnoted Postscript:

On the land and flag God's blessings
Obligated we are
Remembering the dead and the bereaved
In our daily prayers
For this is a time to pray and supplicate.

From 2001 to 2002, I had gathered enough material to complete a novel. The writing of the novel went through many turns and twists, while at the same time, serendipity seemed to have played into my camp. One of those turns and twists which has a moral prominence over the rest, pertains to a woman of conscience. Looking and assessing what that woman of conscience had done to put behind her what is considered the throes of partnership, I started playing with my pen for about a score and five minutes, and thinking that there is a need to mention an innocent-looking princess in my book. Although the novel began its gestation in 1999, it was Lady Diana's tragic death that saddened me to refer to her humble spirit that characterized the milk of her human kindness in *The Melodrama of the Last Word*, published in 2003. Its sub-title is: *Here I am, Send Me*. To her spirit and memory, the novel begins: When it comes to a crunch and as things were badly withering and falling down, Lady Diana asked, "Who shall I send?"

Looking into the innocent eyes of the princess, Jola said, "Here I am, send me." This is how the novel acquires its subtitle.

Believing that the more competitive a society is, the more aggressive and violent its citizens are. On the same pedestal, knowing full well that man has to endure some kind of pain in his journey to becoming a meaningful creature in the world, I began to play down the pain I went through when my brothers and sisters died, when my parents died, when my parents' houses went in flames and when the bloody 21st century disappoints me. If only I could play down those painful experiences, it is then, it is only then would I be able to concentrate on becoming a writer: not just a "closet writer" but a writer of substance. Thus I proceeded to read more and more Commonwealth writers and topping my list is Salman Rushdie.

In no time at all, it occurs to me that the more the mind is at peace, the more productive it will be. Evidently, by the end of 2003, I have a total of fifty titles of literary works. Consequently, I felt as I feel today that had anyone of those "big-time publishers"—the mainstream publishers discovered me on their thresholds, I could have undergone the media rituals of noise-making and then become a prolific writer of substance.

Whenever life is bloody and warlike, I will say to myself that what I have which is immortal is my creative work, produced by my creative mind. But whenever nature is serene and exuberant with life, I will say to myself that nothing do I have but my soul which has gained a spiritual entrance to the realm of immortality.

Complexity interred, obscurity dispelled, it becomes increasingly and distinctly clear from day to day that I cannot divorce my becoming a writer from immortality. Both are seemingly the same. And any attempt to separate them is non sequitur.

Two thousand and four saw the publication of *Literatures of the African Diaspora,* by Gival Press, a small but upbeat independent publishing house. This is my third book after the destruction of the World Trade Center in 2001.

In the book, I referred to *Omeros* by a Nobel Prize Winner, Derek Walcott. I referred to him because he is the first African in Diaspora to lay so much emphasis on the quintessence of having a name with a meaning. Choosing an African-Yoruba name, Afolabi, whose meaning is *born with honor*, he said:

A name means something
The qualities desired in a son
and even a girl child;
so even the shadows who called
you expected one virtue,
since every name is a blessing.

Epigrammatically, professor Walcott has aptly described a name from the Yoruba/African perspective. Thus, he assures Africans in Africa and Africans in Diaspora that he has not forgotten his family tree even if his own African names are in the back burner, marching behind his slave-given names.

Also mentioned in the book is Nelson Mandela—as the man of the 20th century. And while in New Delhi in 1994, I couched the following poem to honor—**the man of the century:**

I salute you
Let's salute him
Man of the century
From fire to fame
From Misunderstanding
to Understanding
From oppression
to expression
I salute you
Man of the Century.

Who else can be saluted?

But you
Who else has suffered
a moonless incarceration?
But you
What else has—
"managed and delighted the world?"
(meaning your cognomen)
But you
Who else has been resurrected?
But you
Man of the Century
I salute you.

The Yoruba's Book of Enlightenment which is otherwise known as Ifa-Ife was under the light of the day in *Literatures of the African Diaspora*. It should not be confused with the Way of Enlightenment which in page 110 of the book, tests the philosophical drive of Man and thusly says, "The Man treading the Way of Enlightenment may stumble and fall many times. He will refuse to be lured into any temptation of defeat while trying to encourage himself and survive the vicissitudes of life. He will remove every obstacle in his way so as to endure the suffering which the vicissitudes of life will place before him, ere he reaches the crest of his mount of destiny. The reward of his manliness will not be based on material acquisition alone. The reward of his manliness will be judged by the Divine Grace which Creator-Philosopher Olodumare has bestowed upon him. He is now a spiritualist who is able to see beyond his nose and able to touch and heal in the name of our omnipresent highest Spirit of our creation."

The reason I am interested in Yoruba philosophy using the Book of Enlightenment is to discover how the unwritten philosophy had helped our ancestors live largely a spiritual life under the Divine Grace during their days as opposed to living largely a material existence under the same Divine Grace in this day and age.

In sum, the Book of Enlightenment under the Divine Grace has tremendously helped me to become a Man who is on his way to becoming a writer of high caliber whose philosophies entail strong moral fiber.

In one of my discourses in the book, I let my fellow writers in English know that most of the writers from the English-speaking countries in colonial Africa and Asia have adopted English (by necessity of communication, education, information and entertainment) as their lingua franca. Majority of these writers (with due respect to my fellow writers) cannot speak fluently let alone write smoothly their mother tongues. English language has become a number one world language and may remain so till the end of time. In sum and substance, it is like splitting an apple into two equal halves of a major premise and a minor premise. The major premise: colonized people speak the language (English) of their colonizers. The minor premise: you are a colonized person. The reasoning conclusion will therefore be, you can speak the language (English) of the colonizers—because you were a colonizer.

Additionally, I remember pointing out that anyone speaking and writing in a language for 25 years at least or 50 years at most has the birthright, similar to, and as likened to major and minor premises, can call such a language—English— his/her mother tongue. He/she is now born in *English*. Therefore he/she is *English*.

Chapter Thirty-Eight

Dyed-in-the-Wool

Even when confidence seems to have removed all the vestiges of doubt and lethargy, and have them buried deep beneath my feet, I still refuse to call myself a writer, fully fledged. I looked at my right, what did I find? I found a table of assignments staring at me. Next, I looked at my left and found a field of hurdles. Was it a shallow dream in a paradoxical sleep? So it seemed. Interpretatively, it meant to be me. Me, I have a job still to do. It becomes lucid both in my corporeal and spiritual consciousness that my "yes" in becoming a writer will require more than how to read, write and pass all the oral and written examinations on the surface of the earth.

I proceeded to say to my alter-ego that I cannot become a professional writer of substance if my writing is not geared to helping the world. By helping the world is to let my writing assume a flowering dimension of touching the hearts of the people in leadership positions who knowingly or unknowingly are bending the moral staff of progress, peace, happiness and co-existence and thus causing pain and death to their fellow human beings: causing more problems to the world.

Additionally, I want my writing to have the ethical or spiritual energy to disarm a youth, for example, who might find himself/herself in an unfortunate situation—holding a Kalashnikov and pointing it at his/her classmates.

To show that I am prepared to take the bull by the horns (and the snake joyfully by the tail), I inserted the following in the 2nd edition of *The Writers and Politics*, published in 2005 by Author Choice, an imprint of I-Universe, Inc:

"There are many political leaders who do not know that they are murderers. They are imbued with a sense of their own importance. It is universally accepted that the purpose of political practice is to reach for peace, happiness and prosperity. A country starts to inflict suffering on peace, happiness and prosperity if the rate of unemployment is very high, and if there are no employment benefits. A country starts to inflict suffering on peace, happiness and prosperity if there is widespread social unrest. A country starts to inflict suffering on peace, happiness and prosperity if there are cases of starvation, and if the citizens start to die of hunger. A country starts to inflict suffering on peace, happiness and prosperity if it goes into a shooting war with another country. Going into a shooting war, means fighting and killing in hundreds and thousands. Whenever this happens, the leaders concerned could be regarded as active murderers. The leaders whose citizens die of political, economic and social unrest and deprivation should be said to be passive killers. Added to this is the fact that if any leader directly or indirectly supports any shooting war, he or she will be regarded as a passive killer."

The second insertion which sarcastically and heartily throws a frown at the Organization of African Unity (OAU), founded in 1963 is:

"There must be a sound philosophical reason to form the OAU. And the sound philosophical reason will inevitably give birth to progress and vitality. The mental poverty of philosophy does not augur well for anything done without a transcendental mind. As a matter of fact, mental poverty of philosophy is the downfall of many associations. To know the philosophy of your continent is to pull yourself out of the quagmire of poverty of thought in which it has found itself.

"One may argue that OAU is not a department of philosophy. Even if it is not a philosophy department, it is nevertheless interested in the philosophy that can usher in progress and vitality. Every OAU player is supposed to be versed in a philosophical ken of accomplishing things, with or without the so-called philosopher's stone. The presence and the application of transcendentalism will lead to the organization's progress and vitality. Its absence will inevitably and unequivocally cause not only its crash to the lowest ebb, but also its demise."

In all the years I have been struggling day and night to become a writer, I have refused to become a writer until a big and wall-shaking noise is made about my writing. I shall take no for an answer. The contents of my gourd will contain no compromise. No going back but forward. Forward ever is the char of my lemon tea.

In 2006, Publish America agreed to publish *The Anthologies of the Diaspora*. Page 119 of the book carries a discourse, under which there is an exordium. It reads, "Since Professor Abimbola's essay on Ifa Divination Poetry in 1970s, I have been laboring to find the origin of the god-send poetry and diviners behind them.

All what the diviners and the scions of the land want me to believe is that the Book of Enlightenment was the Authority of pre-Jesus Christ, so also Ifamas was the festival of the oracles prior to the Christian Era. In short, Christmas was derived from Ifamas which belongs to everything that holds together Ifa Divination Poetry; its beginning and its end; its ontology, hagiology, cosmology and cosmogony.

Ontologically, hagiologists dwell both in heaven and on earth. Among the Orisas, they are the saints. Saints are Orisas, Orisas are saints. They carry messages between heaven and earth. Some theogonists assert that they are angelic philosophers or God's spirits (emi Olorun), acting as intermediaries between Orisas and Olodumare, the Creator-Philosopher.

Back to Ifa again. Ifa is the most important of all the forms of Yoruba oral poetry, the divination corpus. The corpus consists of two hundred and fifty-six branches, known as Odu. Each Odu is like a sermon, steeped in obscurity. It is intricate so much that no one, not even a diviner can tell precisely the number of poems therein—as no one can tell precisely the omnificence and majesty of the existence of the Supreme Being, known as Olodumare, the Philosopher-Creator of heaven and earth.

Compared to the Bible, it is almost four times more voluminous than the sixty-six books in the Holy Writ. As the cosmologists extol its spirituality, so also the cosmogonists exult its heavenliness.

Poring over the eon of oral anthologies, Tai Bola (1898-1989), argued that it was very difficult to imagine that any other oral poetry could be more voluminous, more dramatic, rhetorical, doxological, or richer than Ifa Divination Poetry. Most rhetoricians derive their contextual know-how from Ifa poetry. An Ifa rhetorician can perform twelve hours non-stop. The historian Bola added by saying that there was a "divinatory blood" coursing the veins and arteries of Dr. Martin Luther King, Junior, whenever he opened his mouth to speak.

By and large, Ifa and Ifamas must be as old as the holy city of Ile-Ife, the frist settlement when the Creator-Philosopher God first sent down one of his Orisas on the establishment of the present universe. If Ifa is the Bible of the Yoruba heyday, if Ile-Ife is the first settlement on earth and if indeed poetry had been existing in its present divination corpus, it stands to reason therefore, that Christmas which is a Christian festival commemorating the birth of Jesus Christ, the Incarnation of God's eternally begotten Son, must have been an offshoot of Ifamas.

While Professor Hill is reluctant to imbibe the exposition, wholesale, Professor Idowu perorated that as long as there is no laboratory or archaeological proof to the contrary, etymologists must continue to search for a proven answer.

An aberration, for Divinity-Philosopher Oduduwa's sake: has Ooni of Ile-Ife been recognized the primordial Head of the Yorubaland? Don't ask me, steer. Ask other obas whether they have brotherly and constitutionally acquiesced to have a prime-ministerial Captain to steer the ship of the land.

What now remains a closed book is how Ifa oral poetry has been able to acquire and preserve such a monumental number of literary, linguistic and anthropological chapter and verse in its corpus. The vagaries of human mind from its tabula rasa to its contemporary written form, still is shrouded in conjecture and mystery. According to Immanuel Kant (1724-1804), the human mind never grasps the ultimate nature of reality which neither confirmed, denied nor scientifically demonstrated.

In the meantime, further discourse, adjourned sine die.

My prayer for, my interest in, my dream of, my question on, my craving and passion for immortality has never changed ever since I first fell head over heels in love with the diurnal and nocturnal propensities leading towards the antonym of mortality.

Chapter Thirty-Nine

Statement of My Teaching and Writing Philosophy

From the nature's perspective, dissemination which is today known as teaching is an in-born phenomenon. Parents are inclined by nature to teach their children what to do to become good citizens. Elders also teach the youths how to be responsible in the society. Teaching directly or indirectly seems to be an endless process that occurs everyday in one's life.

My first taste of teaching started in 1974 when my first Poetry Book, *The Trans-Continental Poems* was published. During that time, I had no experience. My teaching was like talking about my book. Nothing more and nothing less, except that I cannot compare what I had in my head then with what I have in my head today.

By 1983, when the Institute of Creative Writing was established, my teaching had gained some height of experience. A novel dimension had surfaced, for I did not only see myself as a teacher but also as a disseminator of knowledge and ideas. I see myself wearing a dashiki of responsibility.

However, it was not until 1989 when I began to ruminate over the philosophy of teaching or teaching philosophy. The upshot of my rumination is the publication in 1991 of *The Literary Philosophy for the Year 2000*. The conspectus of the book challenges literary/creative philosophers to critically consider every situation so that whatever they do is done well, reminding them of what Bertrand Russell said, "To understand an age, or a nation, we must understand its philosophy, and to understand its philosophy, we must ourselves be in some degree philosophers."

Thus my statement of philosophy is to understand my students—know what they intend to accomplish in life. Also, would I make them know me. When students know their teacher, his/her teaching philosophy will be very interesting not only to the students but also to the community. I would make my course competitive and attractive by letting them comprehend how it would usefully affect them in the future.

Scholarly and intellectually, my research file would invariably be updated—searching for new ideas and expanding on the current ones. I would ask my students to always be research-curious, for curiosity is another means to widen one's horizon.

Both the advantaged and disadvantaged students would be treated equally and respectfully. My door would be open and I would be prepared to address their concerns, day or night. I would let them embrace the notion that they are the winners who would never quit, reminding them of the philosophy of determination and determinism.

Thinking critically as with Creative Writing and the philosophy of writing—developmentally, would be on the same footing so that they go to the world—making their marks, and on becoming leaders, they would look back gleefully with pride of accomplishment and revel in the good time—the *good teacher cum student experience* we both shared and cherished together.

Humanistic Principles of Writing: One distinct and obvious contribution of a broadly humanistic methodology to the teaching of writing is that it solves the *wahala* (problem) of what to write about. If the snippets of information are to be reorganized into an effective text are provided by the learner, the *wahala* (problem) of what to write about largely disappears.

More often than not, we tabulate elements from the biographies of several learners, not necessarily in a linguistic form, to serve as the material to be written about. One Gordian knot which is a frustrating element of some language-learning experiences is that one never gets to express oneself—we believe that an important part of the learner motivation lies in freeing this pent-up desire.

A second contribution of a humanistic methodology to the teaching of writing lies in its recognition of the unsuitability of offering learners models of language for them to imitate. There are good and encouraging reasons for believing that a process-related approach to teaching writing is preferable to a model-offering or product-related one.

Science of the Literary Arts: Researches have shown that every learner has some knowledge of what he/she intends to learn or must have known something about what he/she is learning. Science of the literary arts puts it this way: The humanistic methodology by which one learns what one doesn't know as well as portraying what one earlier knows is the science of the literary arts.

Writing as a Deficit Skill: It is not possible to learn what no one knows, as it is not necessary to learn what everyone knows. Thus teaching is about helping one group of people to do what another group can already do. Classroom time should be spent on those elements of a task that are difficult or problematic for learners, but not second nature for experts. Although it is not possible to learn what no one knows, *but by not knowing what's knowable when knowing is worth knowing, means knowledge is acquirable for whose mind is ready for it.* In order to single out those elements for special attention, therefore, it must be worth asking precisely what is difficult about writing, and specifically, about writing a book.

Creative Writing: *Creating a Book:* this is where Creative Writing (the writing that is born out of imaginations and harvested from dreams) comes in. Having ideas and having the will-power to write about them is the beginning about the joy and pain of becoming a Creative Writer. And putting these ideas together in a book form, makes one an author—a published author.

Like most stories, my stories are designed to educate, inform, enlighten, inspire, entertain, and above all, inoculate the body with the ingredient of life. And through the course of my writing under the auspices of Creator-Philosopher Olodumare, I have realized how powerful **a word** or **words** can be. Words have their own spiritual energy and that is why a story from a honest mouth has the positive energy to heal physically and spiritually.

Whether writing a fiction or non-fiction, writing a book is onerous and time-consuming. As attested to by George Orwell, "Writing a book is painful. One would never undertake such a thing if one were not driven on by some demon whom one can neither resist nor understand."

Within the realm of Creative Writing are literary philosophy and creative philosophy. They are the same—falling within the same premise. They both derive their recourses from the figments of imaginations and dreams—fashioning and charting the course. Both are the same as narrative philosophy except that a narrative philosophy takes its wefts and warps, facts and figures from the ancients into the hold of the present. This is very vivid in Yoruba philosophy which is essentially a folk philosophy explicating and pointing to the knowledge of the causes and the nature of things, affecting the corporeal and the spiritual universe—and its wellness, un-wellness, joys and sorrows.

If I should place my principles over expediencies, if I should place my serendipity upon platitude, this memoir could not have been written without immortality sitting resplendently upon mortality. Now let me build them into a gate-legged table. On the table are the two fountain-pens used to couch this memoir. They are twisted, badly twisted to the point of breaking. But they are not broken: never can they be broken through the Grace of God. I will keep them for the second and the last BOOK—my MEMOIR.

Now, a mature man, wearing a dashiki of happiness, with *one invisible sense* and five visible senses, I start to wonder whether I am a bringer of light, a keeper of traditions and a learner of the Book of Enlightenment.

(It was towards the end of 2003 that news came to me from Vienna, Austria that my books, about 10 copies in BOOK WORLD, a bookstore, owned and operated by the Afro-Asian Institute had been destroyed. Letters were sent to the bookstore for explanation but there is no reply till this day.)

Reflection

Hear me, Oh Creator-Philosopher Olodumare, vouchsafe that my words, as my unspoken words tickle the bosoms of one and all, and din in the ears of every soul who will like to know the circumstances leading to *The Birth of a Child in a Fishing Boat,* which is born at the beginning of a sentence which reads, *nothing is impossible when a heart is set to it.*

I hope, I believe this unique autobiography/memoir, first of its kind from the Yoruba Atlantic, will shed light on how the natural medicines (in the absence of the modern medicines) are able to save the lives of many (in the 1950s) living in the littoral towns and villages, infested with many tropical diseases.

The medicine of our time has combated a large department of the causes of human diseases. Thus the import of this reflection is that the child boy is a combatant, a survivor and he has every reason to enter the department of gratitude, enjoyment and felicity, initiated and authorized by Creator-Philosopher Olodumare.

Printed in the United States
By Bookmasters